Elsie

the

Outsider

BRECK CAMPBELL

ISBN 979-8-35097-456-0 ebook 979-8-35097-457-7

Acknowledgements

This book would not have been possible without help from a few important people. First, I would like to thank my Mom and Dad for encouraging me to author Elsie's/my own story. Gabrielle Mistretta, for letting me bounce ideas off you during our workouts. Zoey Laster for an amazing cover design. Finally, I would like to thank Jennifer Molaison, who is undoubtedly the best editor a first-time author had the good luck to stumble across.

Chapter 1

Belly Full of Butterflies

Elsie woke up out of a deep sleep, but she could not figure out what had woken her up. There was no light on in the room. At least, she assumed there was no light in the room; even if there *had* been any light, she could not see it. Elsie had never been able to see the light because she was born blind.

People always asked her if she saw black, and she could not give them an answer. For ten years, all she had known was what she called "nothingness." People could not understand that she did not know what black was, so she could not tell them if she was seeing it. Everyone said that when they closed their eyes, they saw black. *If people saw black when it was dark, did that mean she saw black all the time*? She did not know and did not really care. Her standard answer was always "*I see nothing.*"

She reached for her iPhone to check the time. She had just gotten the phone for Christmas, and she loved that it talked to her. Elsie groaned when her phone told her that it was only 3:00 A.M. At least she had the phone; in the past, when she had woken up in the night like this, she had not realized how early it was.

Grandma Sally always liked to tell people about a time when she was three and had woken up early. Grandma Sally always laughed when she said, "It was 2:00 AM, and Elsie was wide awake and wanted to play. It did not matter to her that it was still dark outside. I put her in bed with me and let her play with her toys, and she was as happy as could be."

Elsie remembered that her favorite toy when she was little had been a fluffy duck that made a cheeping sound. Elsie thought it was funny when

Grandpa George got annoyed with the duck cheeping. He always yelled, "Kill the duck!"

She had also loved how soft and fluffy it was. She could remember rubbing the fluffy duck against her cheek to feel its softness. Now, she snuggled her teddy bear instead and wished that it were not a school day. If she did not have school, she would get out of bed now, and take a nap later when she got tired.

Thinking about school made her belly feel queasy. It trembled like a bowl of butterflies. She got up after all and went to her parents' bedroom to tell her mom she felt sick.

"Mom?" She shook her mom's shoulder.

Mom stirred in bed. "Elsie, what's wrong?"

Elsie heard her dad cough and roll over in his sleep. "My belly hurts," she said.

Mom slowly got up out of bed and walked Elsie back to her bedroom. Elsie climbed into bed and snuggled her favorite teddy bear. When she was comfortable, Mom pulled the covers up over her and kissed the top of her head.

"Your belly is fine," Mom said. "You're just worried about tomorrow. Stop worrying and go to sleep. When you wake up, you'll feel just fine."

Elsie heard her mom walk back to her own bedroom and get into bed. She had hoped her mom would say that since her belly hurt, she could take an extra day off school. Tomorrow would be the first day back after Christmas break. And thinking about tomorrow made her think about the week of school *before* the break. The week before Christmas break, her class had cut out construction paper Christmas trees to tape to their desks on the day of the party. When Elsie was handed hers, it just felt like a plain piece of paper. Her aide, Mrs. Perry, had taken the paper and put Wikki Stix on the paper in the shape of a tree; the Wikki Stix, which felt like sticky chenille pipe cleaners, let Elsie feel the outline of the tree and cut around it.

Elsie hated using scissors because she could not see where she was cutting. She had to use her fingers to feel the outline of the tree, and she was always afraid that she would cut herself.

When she accidentally cut into the tree, Mrs. Perry, and the classroom teacher Mrs. Conklin, had gotten mad at her.

"Now I'll have to put Wikki Stix on another tree," Mrs. Perry had said as she grabbed the broken tree off Elsie's desk.

Mrs. Conklin sighed. "Since Mrs. Perry will have to spend her time putting Wikki Stix on another tree, you'll have to stay in during recess and cut it out."

Elsie rested her elbow on the desk and put her chin in her hand. It embarrassed her to get in trouble in front of the class. She hated sitting awkwardly, waiting for Mrs. Perry to finish putting Wikki Stix on the new tree. She did not understand why cutting out a tree was so important anyway. It was supposed to be a treat to stop classwork and do craft. *But what good was craft when you could not see?*

She thought maybe if the craft had not involved scissors and cutting, she might have enjoyed it. She liked playing with Wikki Stix when they were not being used to help her cut something. Mrs. Perry said they reminded her of Twizzlers. Elsie agreed that they did feel a bit like Twizzlers; they were sticky and ropey, just like the candy. When Mrs. Perry finished the new tree, Elsie cut very slowly so she would not make a mistake. But even though she tried hard to cut out the new tree, she still had not finished at the end of the day.

The next day had been the Christmas party, and her teachers had not made her work on the tree again. She had not cared that she was the only kid without a tree taped to the front of her desk.

Now, snuggled into her warm covers, Elsie hoped that her first day back after Christmas break would be a good one. As she drifted off to sleep her last thought was a prayer: "*Dear God, thank you for a new day tomorrow, and I ask you to bless it.*"

Chapter 2
Why Can't We Be Friends?

The next morning when Elsie woke up, she realized she had overslept.

"You're going to have to hurry to get ready!" Mom said as she shook her awake.

Elsie dressed in the clothes her mom had laid out for her, ate a Pop Tart, and brushed her hair and teeth. When her mom and her little brother, Blake, were ready to go, they got in the car and drove Blake to their babysitter, Linda's house. Mom opened the door to get Blake out of the car, and he said, "I want to give sissy a kiss first!"

"I don't want a kiss," Elsie said.

Blake started to cry, and Mom sighed. "Elsie, just let him give you a kiss."

Elsie grudgingly turned toward Blake and let him give her a kiss on the cheek.

"Bye-bye Sissy," he said.

"Bye, Blake," she answered.

When Mom got back in the car she asked, "Why were you so mean to Blake? You know he's only three."

"I wasn't trying to be mean," Elsie protested. "It's just sometimes his kisses are slobbery and gross."

"He's three years old. Your kisses were slobbery and gross when you were three."

"They were?" Elsie asked in surprise.

"That's just the way kisses from little kids are."

Elsie felt bad for the way she had treated Blake. She loved her brother, but sometimes she still wished she had a sister instead. Elsie had always wanted to have a sister to play dress-up and house with. Often, she felt like she was not sure how to play with Blake. Blake played house sometimes, but it just was not the same playing house with him as it was playing with her cousins Faith and Hope.

Elsie sighed. "I'll tell him sorry later tonight."

"He will not remember what happened," Mom comforted. "Just do better next time."

When they reached the school and Elsie got out of the car, Mrs. Lester was there to meet her. Mrs. Lester was an aide at the school in charge of the kids before school in the morning. She met Elsie at the car so she could guide her to her classmates in the gym, where all the kids gathered every morning to wait for school to start.

"Hi Elsie, how was your Christmas break?" she asked.

"It was good," Elsie said. "I had lots of fun singing in the Christmas program and helping my grandma bake cookies." As they walked into the gym, she could hear the murmur of the other children's voices.

"That sounds like fun," said Mrs. Lester. "Now, I am going to sit you by Amy and Krista so that you can talk to them."

Elsie heard the swish of Amy's coat as she scooted over so Elsie could sit between them. Elsie was excited to tell them about getting a new phone for Christmas, but when she sat down, Amy and Krista were in the middle of a conversation.

"I went out of town to visit my grandparents for Christmas," Krista was saying. "My grandparents live out in the country, and do not have good internet. That's why I couldn't talk to you much."

"That's okay," Amy said. "I just wanted to show you pictures of my new puppy, Princess." Elsie heard Amy unzip her backpack and take out her phone. "I have some pictures on my phone."

Elsie felt Amy reach across her to hand Krista her phone. "She's so cute!" Krista squealed. Then Krista again reached across Elsie to hand the phone to Amy. Elsie heard Amy put the phone back in her backpack and zip it up.

"I got a new phone for—" Elsie tried to say, but Amy kept talking.

"Oh, Krista, you will have to come over and see Princess sometime."

Elsie wondered if they could not hear her. That had to be why they talked over her. *They would not just ignore her, would they?* Amy and Krista were best friends, and Elsie wanted to be friends with them as well. She imagined what it would be like to go to Amy's house. They would play with Princess, and Amy's mom would make them hot chocolate and chocolate-chip cookies. Elsie hoped that if she spent enough time with Amy and Krista, they would accept her as their friend.

"I got a new phone for Christmas," she said when there was a gap in the conversation. "It talks, so I can text people now, and I have a Facebook account!"

Amy's long hair brushed Elsie's arm as the other girl turned toward her. "Wow! I did not know they made phones for people like you. Why would you want to be on Facebook? Most people post pictures on Facebook, and you can't see pictures."

"I don't have a phone made especially for me," Elsie explained. "I have an iPhone. iPhones have voices on them that can talk to you. I like to read what people post with their pictures."

"I don't post any captions with my pictures," Amy said.

"I think there is a way for you to add descriptions to your pictures."

"I don't have time to describe pictures." Amy's voice sounded irritated. "I just post them when Princess does something cute or funny or when I am taking a selfie. When I take a selfie, I'm usually in a hurry and getting ready to go somewhere, so I don't have time to describe the picture."

"I know that I won't be able to see your pictures, but can we be friends on Facebook?" Elsie asked.

Amy sighed. "I'll add you when I get home."

Krista touched Elsie's arm and said, "I'll add you too."

Elsie was excited that Amy and Krista were going to friend her on Facebook. She was one step closer to being accepted by them.

Chapter 3
A New Fashion Style

When the bell rang for the start of the day, everyone got quiet and waited to be dismissed. When Mrs. Lester dismissed the fifth-grade class, Elsie stood up and took Krista's elbow so she could guide her out of the gym. Krista or another classmate always helped Elsie out of the gym because the floor was still crowded, and she did not want to hit anyone with her cane. But once they were in the hallway, Elsie unfolded her cane.

She had been told that her cane looked like a stick, and she understood why. It was shaped kind of like a stick, with a rubber handle for her to hold on top, and a metal tip on the bottom that would survive being tapped and scraped across hardwood floors and concrete.

She tapped her cane on the floor and found the wall. Once she found the wall, she tapped her cane in front of her as she walked to make sure that there was nothing on the ground that she would trip over. She hated walking in the hall in the morning, because there were so many kids that it was hard to avoid hitting someone with her cane. Most people moved away from the wall when they saw her coming, but sometimes when people were at their lockers, they did not see her until she hit their foot with her cane.

Elsie stopped at her own locker to put away her backpack and coat before walking into the classroom. Inside, Mrs. Conklin was trying to get everyone's attention.

"Okay, everyone, settle down. Christmas break is over, and it is time to get back to work. I want you all to write about what you did over the break. When everyone is finished, you will each read aloud what you wrote."

Elsie heard a few kids groan as everyone grabbed paper and pencils. Elsie had a tray on her desk that was filled with her own paper. She used a special kind of paper that was longer and thicker than regular notebook paper. It was strong enough that it would not break when the braille writer punched holes in it. The braille writer left bumps on the page that Elsie could feel. She sat with her hands over the six keys that made up every letter of the alphabet and thought about what to write.

While she wrote, Elsie heard Mrs. Perry walk into the room. "Good morning, Mrs. Conklin," the aide said.

"Good morning, Mrs. Perry. Did you have a good break?"

"Yes, how about you?"

"It was good," Mrs. Perry said. Her shoes squeaked on the floor as she walked over to Elsie's desk, squatted down, and whispered, "Do you know that your shirt is on inside-out?"

Elsie was so embarrassed that she wished the floor would open up and swallow her whole. Although Mrs. Perry had whispered, she had not whispered softly enough because Elsie heard Amy laugh. She knew it was Amy because Amy always snorted when she laughed. Elsie wondered how much snot Amy swallowed every time she laughed.

Elsie felt her face getting warm, and she had to swallow hard to keep tears out of her eyes. She wanted Amy and Krista to like her, but now they would be embarrassed to have her as a friend.

Mrs. Perry told her, "You need to go to the bathroom and fix your shirt."

She thought fast. She did not want to admit that she did not know how to fix her shirt, so she said, "I think it is one of those reversible shirts."

"Sweaters like that aren't reversible."

Elsie licked her lips; her mouth felt suddenly dry. "Can I leave it the way it is? I could start a new fashion trend."

Mrs. Perry laughed. "No. You need to go to the bathroom and fix it."

"Well, um…" Elsie swallowed hard. "I don't know how to fix it."

She heard Amy snort-laugh again at that.

"Come on," Mrs. Perry said, "I'll show you how."

When they walked out of the room, Elsie could not hold back the tears anymore. "I'm sorry. I know how to dress myself. I just never learned how to turn my shirt right-side out."

Mrs. Perry stopped walking and touched Elsie's shoulder. "It's okay. This is a good learning experience. Asking to start a new fashion trend was funny."

Elsie sniffed and wiped her eyes with the sleeve of her sweater. "Now Amy and Krista won't want to be my friend because I'm the weird girl who doesn't know her shirt is on inside-out."

Mrs. Perry sighed. "Your true friends will laugh *with* you, not at you. Come on, let us get your shirt fixed so you can finish writing about your Christmas break."

Back in the classroom, Elsie finished writing about the Christmas program at church and helping Grandma Sally bake cookies. She also wrote about getting an iPhone for Christmas. Elsie hoped that, by writing about getting an iPhone for Christmas, she would help her classmates see her as person just like them. There were many times when Elsie did not feel included, she often felt like an outsider looking in.

After the class shared what they did over Christmas break, everyone put their papers in the assignment basket. Elsie handed her paper to Mrs. Perry so that she could write in print what Elsie brailed.

Later in the afternoon Elsie met with Laura, her occupational therapist. Laura had taught her how to do things like hold a fork and spoon and tie her shoes. Somehow, Laura had found out about Elsie not knowing how to turn her shirt inside-in.

"We are going to work on taking your sweater off and putting it back on," she said.

Elsie was surprised. "How do you know about that?"

"Mrs. Perry told me about it during lunch. Take off your sweater so I can show you how to tell the difference between the inside and outside."

Elsie took off her sweater and shivered. It was cold in the therapy room, and the T-shirt she wore under her sweater had short sleeves.

Laura took Elsie's hand and put it on her sweater. "Do you feel this? It's smooth." Elsie heard rustling and then Laura put her hand on the shirt again. "Now I turned it inside-out. Do you feel the stitching?"

"Yes. It feels rougher."

"Those are the stitches on the inside of your shirt. When you feel this, it means your shirt is inside-out. To make sure your shirt is right-side out, you are going to reach into your shirt and pull the outside of your shirt out while you push the inside-in." Laura showed Elsie how to do it, and then made Elsie try to do it by herself. When she successfully turned her shirt right-side out several times, Laura let her put it back on.

"I always encourage all the kids I work with to reach for the stars. If you want to become an influencer, I support you but try to think of a better reason to influence things around you other than not knowing how to do something."

Elsie was not sure how she felt. *Was this what Mrs. Perry meant about people laughing with her*? She guessed it was kind of funny, but she wondered if Amy had laughed with her or *at* her this morning.

Chapter 4
Questions About Blindness

At the end of the day, Elsie got on the bus and sat in her usual seat right behind the driver. She had just scooted over to the window when she felt someone plop down in the seat beside her.

"Hi, I'm Shaylyn. You are Elsie, right? I am new here. My classmates pointed you out at recess and said that you were blind."

Elsie wished that there was something memorable about her aside from being blind. She hated that when people pointed her out or introduced her, her blindness was always the first thing they said about her.

"Hi, Shaylyn. Yes, I am Elsie," she said.

Elsie could feel the other girl shift in the seat as she took off her backpack. When she had placed it under her seat Shaylyn asked, "Is it true that you're blind? You don't *look* blind."

Elsie had never understood what sighted people thought about blind people. "What do you think blind people look like?"

Shaylyn squirmed and rubbed her hands together. She was quiet for so long that Elsie wondered if she would ever answer, but finally she said, "You know . . . most blind people wear glasses, or don't have any eyes. Sometimes their eyes look funny or are small. Your eyes look normal, and you're not wearing glasses."

Elsie was silent for a moment. She wondered where the idea that blind people must *look* blind came from. "There are some blind people who have really small eyes or wear glasses, but others don't," she told Shaylyn.

"Why are you blind?"

Elsie started picking at her nails and did not answer right away. She always found it hard to explain to kids her age why she was blind.

Shaylyn touched her arm. "I'm sorry. My mom is always telling me I should think before I speak. I didn't mean to hurt your feelings."

Elsie sighed. "You didn't hurt my feelings, but I have a hard time explaining to other people why I'm blind. It is kind of weird. My eyes are fine. My optic nerve is the problem."

"What's an optic nerve?"

"Your optic nerve is a nerve connected to the brain and your eyes that tells your brain what you're seeing. My optic nerve is too small."

Shaylyn was silent for a minute. "So, since your optic nerve thing is too small, it can't tell your brain what your eyes are seeing?"

"Yes. The way my dad explains it, he says that seeing is like three people working together. The eye, the optic nerve, and the brain are three people, but if one of them does not do their part, then the others cannot either. My optic nerve is too small to do its part, so my brain doesn't know what my eyes are seeing."

Shaylyn thought about this for a minute. "That makes sense. Do you like to feel people's faces? You can feel my face if you want to," she offered, and then took Elsie's hand and put it on her face.

"I don't like feeling people's faces," Elsie said. "I think it's kind of yucky."

Shaylyn dropped Elsie's hand and scooted as far away from Elsie as she could in the tiny seat. "I'm not yucky. I wash my face every morning."

Elsie realized that she had spoken before she thought it through. "I didn't mean *you* are yucky. I just meant that it is kind of yucky to touch people's faces because we all have a lot of germs on our hands. And it isn't good to touch your own face, so touching someone else's face must be even worse."

Shaylyn turned back toward Elsie. "That makes sense. My mom always tells me not to touch my face. Can I tell you what I look like?"

"Sure," Elsie agreed.

"I am just a bit taller than you. I have curly red hair and green eyes. I know you do not like touching faces, but would you like to feel my hair?"

Elsie loved playing with other people's hair but was always too shy to ask if she could. "Sure," she said again.

Shaylyn took her hand and put it on her hair. Elsie ran her fingers through the other girl's hair and then put her hand back in her lap. She did not know anyone that had hair like Shaylyn's.

"Wow, it's very curly. I like it."

Shaylyn sighed. "My sister likes to pat my head like a dog and call me 'fluffy.'" She picked up a few strands of Elsie's hair. "You have really pretty light brown hair. My sister has hair kind of like yours, except hers is thicker. I always tell her that her hair is like a horse's tail."

Elsie laughed at that thought. "Thank you."

Shaylyn put down the strands of Elsie's hair she had been playing with and bent to pick up her backpack. "We're almost at my stop. Can I sit with you again sometime?"

"I won't be on the bus tomorrow," Elsie told her. "But you can on Wednesday."

"Why won't you be on the bus tomorrow?"

"I have to work with Julie. She's a teacher for kids who are blind and visually impaired."

"What does she teach you?" Shaylyn asked. Before Elsie could answer she said, "Am I asking too many questions? My mom says I ask too many questions."

"I don't mind you asking. Julie taught me how to read braille and use a cane when I was younger. Now we work on crossing streets and using computers."

"Wow! You can use a computer?"

"Yes," Elsie said. "Some computers can talk, and now we have computers that have braille displays. A braille display is kind of like a screen except it has braille, not print.""

When the bus stopped, Shaylyn touched Elsie's arm and asked, "See you Wednesday?"

"Sure."

After Shaylyn left, Elsie thought about their conversation. She did ask a *lot* of questions, but not in a mean way. Elsie did not mind answering her questions and found that she kind of liked having someone to sit with.

*

When Elsie and her family sat down to dinner that night, Dad asked, "How was everyone's day?"

Elsie took a bite of peas and said, "I accidentally went to school with my shirt on inside-out, and when Mrs. Perry told me I was wearing it wrong, I tried to say that it was one of those reversible sweaters."

Elsie's dad laughed, and then choked on the bite of food he was chewing.

"That's what you get for laughing at our daughter," Mom joked.

Dad continued to laugh and said, "Shirts like that aren't reversible."

"That's what Mrs. Perry said. I was embarrassed because I didn't know how to fix it, so I asked if I could start a new fashion trend."

Her dad laughed even harder. "Honey, how did you not know that your daughter's sweater was on inside-out?" he asked his wife.

Mom sighed. "I'm sorry, Elsie. I was so stressed this morning. I knew today would be a hard day at work and I was thinking about that instead of looking to make sure you were dressed right."

Elsie knew that Mom worked at a counseling office. She had often heard her mom say that she did not like her boss, Marsha. Mom had talked about disagreements that Marsha, and her other boss, Pam, had had over the years. Elsie wondered if today was so stressful because they had another fight. She wished that they would get along so her mom's job would be easier.

"Mom, what made today so stressful?"

Mom sighed. "Marsha just got back from vacation, and she had a lot of people that were trying to get an appointment. We also have a lot of new clients, and it can be hard scheduling them for their first appointment."

"Why is it hard scheduling people for their first appointment?"

"A lot of them are nervous about talking to someone for the first time. Some of them get so nervous that they don't show up, and that makes Marsha angry because that is time that she could have been with another client, and time she won't be paid for."

"What about Pam?"

"Pam is more understanding. She knows how hard it can be, trying to talk to someone for the first time."

"You like Pam, don't you?" Elsie asked as she chased a potato around her plate with her fork.

"Yes, I like Pam. If Marsha weren't there, I would really like my job."

Part of Elsie wished that Marsha would quit so her mom would like her job, but she was afraid that if Marsha left, Pam would as well, and she did not want Mom to not have a job.

Elsie heard the ice clink in Dad's cup as he took a drink and said, "I guess Marsha's vacation didn't make her feel better?"

Elsie heard a crunch as Mom bit into her meat. "No. I think it made her feel worse because she knows how hard the holiday season is for many of her clients, and she feels like she abandoned them."

"Mom, I'm sorry you had a rough day," Elsie told her.

"Thanks honey," Mom said in a tired voice. "I'm sorry I didn't realize your shirt was on wrong before we left."

Elsie hated that her mom thought she had to make sure she was dressed right every morning. "I'm sorry *I* didn't realize my shirt was on inside-out."

Mom sighed again and took a drink. "It's not your fault. I never thought to teach you that. I taught you how to get dressed, but I never thought to teach you how to tell when your clothes were inside-out."

"Mrs. Perry helped me fix it, and Laura showed me how to turn my shirts right-side out."

"That's good. I'm glad they helped you."

Elsie continued eating her dinner and listened to Blake talk about his day at Linda's house.

"Today Mrs. Linda told me and the other kids that are going to preschool next year that we needed to be good friends to make friends," he said.

Blake talking about making new friends made Elsie think of Shaylyn. "I had something else weird happen today," she said.

"Your brother is talking," Dad reminded her.

Elsie finished the last of the food on her plate while she waited for Blake to finish talking. *Why did it take so long to talk about making new friends at preschool?* Finally, Blake was finished, and Dad turned to Elsie.

"So, what else was weird about today?" he asked.

"It was not weird, it was just . . . different. A new girl sat by me on the bus, and she started asking questions about blindness."

She heard her dad stand up. Plates clanked and clattered as he stacked his plate on top of hers, and then dumped both plates and forks into the sink. "What's so different about that?" Dad asked. "Kids ask you questions about being blind all the time."

"The questions were weird. She was asking me things like if I want to feel her face, and why don't I wear glasses?"

Elsie heard Mom take more plates to the sink and turn on the water. "You said she's new?"

"Yeah, she said her family just moved here. A classmate pointed me out to her at recess. Why is my blindness the most important thing about me?" Elsie stood and walked over to the sink to help with the dishes.

Dad handed her a dirty plate and said, "It's not the most important thing about you; it's just the first thing people remember. You are the only blind person they know. The other kids in your grade do not ask you many questions anymore because they have grown up with you, but Shaylyn is new to town and has not grown up with you. You are probably fascinating to her. I'm sure the only things she knows about blind people is what she sees on TV and reads in books."

"But there aren't many TV shows or books about blind people. Maybe she's read something about Helen Keller or watched *The Miracle Worker*." Elsie dunked the plate in the soapy water and scraped at some crusted-on food.

Mom said, "Her parents or grandparents might like Ray Charles or Stevie Wonder. You know your grandpa likes them."

She handed the plate to her mom and said, "I forgot about them. Anyway, for a second I thought I might have hurt her feelings. When she asked me if I wanted to feel her face, I said that touching someone's face was yucky."

Dad handed her the next plate and asked, "What did she say?"

Elsie washed the plate as she answered. "She told me her face wasn't yucky cause she washed it every morning. I explained that we had lots of germs on our hands and that's why touching faces was yucky."

Mom took the wet plate from her and said, "You handled that well. Did Shaylyn understand?"

"She said she understood. She asked me if I wanted to feel her hair, and I did. It is curly and fluffy. But why do people assume I want to feel their faces?"

Dad handed Elsie the next plate. "She's probably seen something on TV or read a book where blind people like to feel faces," he said.

She sighed. "It was hard explaining why I am blind. She understood, and she seems like a nice girl. When she asked if she could sit with me again, I told her she could."

Her mom finished putting the dishes away and ruffled Elsie's hair. "It would be good for you to have a new friend."

"Amy and Krista are my friends," Elsie argued.

Her dad kissed her on the top of her head and said, "You can never have too many friends."

Chapter 5
Dodgeball

The next day at school was a PE day. Elsie *hated* PE. Usually, she was left out of whatever they were playing. When she was allowed to play, the instructor put her on a team and gave her a ball to throw every now and then. Today they were playing dodgeball, and Mr. Wexler, the coach, decided to let her play this time.

As much as Elsie wanted to be like everyone else, she hated dodgeball, and wished that it were one of the many games Mr. Wexler said was too dangerous for her. She guessed the only reason Mr. Wexler let her play was because he did not have to do much to help her, and the balls were soft, so he did not worry about her getting hurt.

Elsie felt like this made her stand out more than if he had told her that it was too dangerous for her to play. At least other kids had to sit out occasionally. She remembered how one of the kids in her class last year had to sit out because of a sprained ankle. Elsie and the girl had talked while everyone else played soccer. No one else just stood around and waited for someone to hand them a ball.

Mr. Wexler patted her on the shoulder and said, "I'll put you on a team, and you can throw the first ball of the game."

When he finished dividing the class into teams, he handed Elsie a dodgeball and announced, "Elsie will throw the first ball of the game. Once she throws her ball, the rest of you may start playing."

Elsie took a deep breath and threw the ball as hard as she could. She did not hear where the ball landed because once it left her hand, the gym filled with the sounds of running, screaming, and bouncing balls. She did not try to join the game; she hated dodgeball. Kids ran everywhere, and no one watched where they were going. She was afraid that someone would run into her and knock her over.

She was lost in her own thoughts, wondering what songs they would learn in their next choir rehearsal, when she felt a ball bounce off her forehead. Thankfully, the ball was soft and did not hurt.

"What's the point of playing dodgeball if you can't dodge the ball?" a classmate shouted.

The rest of the students laughed, and Elsie sighed. She was not sure who said it but knew Mr. Wexler would not do anything about it. She was sure that Mr. Wexler *knew* that people were being bullied, but that he was too lazy to care. She decided that him not caring who got bullied was the one way in which she was treated equally in Mr. Wexler's class.

Although Mr. Wexler did not care who was bullied, he did care when people did not play fair. She knew she was 'out' and should go stand on the sidelines with the rest of the kids who were out, but she did not know how to get there.

"I'm out," she called. "Can someone help me go stand on the sidelines?"

Elsie did not think anyone had heard her, and she did not know what to do. She wanted to play fairly, but she was afraid to move out of her corner and get knocked down by one of her classmates. She was still wondering what to do when Mr. Wexler handed her another ball. "Throw straight ahead and you will hit someone," he said.

"I got hit with a ball," she told him. "I'm out."

"It's okay, go ahead and throw the ball," he said.

To Elsie's surprise, when she threw the ball, she hit someone.

"Hey that's not fair!" another student shouted. "She's supposed to be out!"

Elsie had to agree with the kid. It was not fair that she got to throw a ball when she was supposed to be out. For the rest of the PE period, Elsie wondered if the reason Mr. Wexler did not treat her fairly was because she was blind.

Elsie was quite sure that Mrs. Perry knew about how Mr. Wexler treated her because she and her parents had talked about it, and they had told Mrs. Perry. She guessed that Mrs. Perry had talked to him about it at some point because he got better for a couple weeks, and then went back to his old ways. Elsie did not want to say anything about it again because she did not think it would do any good.

Besides, she would not have to deal with him ever again after the end of the year. She would be going to the middle school, and she had heard a rumor that he was retiring. Elsie thought that if the rumor was true, it was probably for the best. In her opinion he had always been lazy, but it had gotten worse this year. She was thankful that she would only have to put up with him for a few more months.

She was doubly thankful when he blew the whistle for the end of the game. Elsie's team had won but no one seemed incredibly happy.

While they washed their hands before lunch, Elsie heard someone walk to the sink beside her. Krista said, "It's lucky you were on our team. If you had not hit Dylan with that ball, we would have lost for sure."

Elsie decided that if there was one good thing about the dodgeball game, it was that she and Krista had something to talk about. She was happy that Krista had come over to talk to her without a teacher seating them together. Elsie sometimes wondered if the only reason Amy and Krista talked to her in the mornings was because Mrs. Lester sat her with them.

Elsie sighed. "I shouldn't have been allowed to throw that ball. I was out, and I told Mr. Wexler."

Krista touched Elsie's arm and said, "I know, I heard you tell Mr. Wexler that you were out."

Elsie was happy that Krista was talking to her and wanted to keep the conversation going. She grabbed a paper towel and said, "I think that Mr.

Wexler didn't do anything because he is lazy. It was easier for him to give me another ball than to help me stand on the sidelines. I have heard that he is going to retire. If that is true, it is a good thing."

Krista laughed. "Yes, he is going to retire. My mom's on the PTA, and she says they are planning a retirement party for him."

Elsie wiped her hands and kicked out with her foot to find the trash can. She knew it was beside the sink, but she always liked to kick it with her foot so she could make sure she got the paper towel in the trash and not on the floor.

"He's so lazy," Elsie said. "Does he even deserve a party?"

Krista laughed and threw her own paper towel away. "My mom says that he was her gym teacher, and that he was a lot of fun back then. She says that he has been sick for the past few years."

Elsie felt bad that she had thought so many mean thoughts about Mr. Wexler, but she was also worried about what Krista would think about her. "Oh, I didn't know."

"I said the same thing to my mom when she told me about the party. She doesn't know what's wrong with him; she just knows he's sick."

Elsie was glad that she and Krista had the same thought. It made her feel better to know that others felt the same way about Mr. Wexler.

Krista opened the bathroom door, and Elsie tried to make sure she did not hit Krista's foot with her cane as she walked out. She would hate to ruin a new friendship by hitting Krista's foot.

As Krista walked away, she said, "I'll make sure Amy and I sit with you at lunch."

Elsie wanted to do a happy dance down the hall, but she was worried about what people would think of her if she did. She was happy that Amy and Krista were chasing to sit with her.

Chapter 6
The School for the Blind

When Elsie got to the cafeteria, she left her cane in the corner by the door. Mrs. Lester always helped Elsie get her tray, so she did not need it to get around the busy room. Elsie was allowed to cut in line because if she did not, she was always at the back of the line. The halls were crowded at lunchtime, and because Elsie was afraid of hitting people with her cane, she walked slowly. This meant that, by the time she got to where the line was forming, she was at the back of it. By the time the kids at the back of the line got their trays, lunch was half over. Elsie was not a fast eater, so her parents, Mrs. Perry, and Julie decided that she should be the first one to get her tray so she would have time to eat.

"Hi Elsie," Mrs. Lester touched her arm. "What did you order for lunch today?"

"I ordered the beef stroganoff."

"That's your favorite, isn't it?"

"Yes," Elsie agreed. She took Mrs. Lester's elbow, and the older woman guided Elsie to the counter where the beef stroganoff was being served. Elsie heard the "plop" as the cook spooned beef stroganoff onto her tray.

"Would you like green beans?" the cook asked.

"Yes please," Elsie answered, and there was another "plop" as the green beans landed on her tray. She hoped the *plop* meant they were not crunchy. Elsie hated when green beans were crunchy.

Once her tray was filled, Elsie took Mrs. Lester's elbow, and the teacher grabbed Elsie's tray. Mrs. Lester always carried Elsie's tray because

Elsie had a tough time balancing a full tray of food. The few times Elsie had tried, she ended up spilling food on her clothes.

When they got to the milk coolers, Mrs. Lester asked, "Would you like white or chocolate milk today?"

"Chocolate."

"It's in the cooler on your left."

Elsie reached out and found the coolers. She felt for the cooler on her left and opened it and got a chocolate milk. Once she got her milk, she took Mrs. Lester's elbow again and they walked to the table where her class sat.

She had just taken the first bite when she heard someone sit in the chair beside her.

"Hi Elsie," said Amy. "Krista and I were wondering if you want to swing with us at recess?"

"Sure, I'd love to!" Elsie exclaimed. She heard someone pull out the chair on her other side and guessed it was Krista.

"We know you swing most days, and we thought you might want to swing with some friends," Amy continued. Elsie was excited. *Was this that for which she had been waiting? Were Amy and Krista finally accepting her as a friend?*

"Why do you like to swing so much?" Krista asked through a mouth full of food.

"Krista, don't talk with your mouth full, that's gross," Amy said.

Elsie finished her milk and answered, "I wouldn't be any good at jumping rope and playing ball. But I like swinging; it feels like flying."

"That makes sense," Krista said. "Are you ready to put your tray away?"

"Yes."

Amy stood up and said, "Come on, you can walk with me."

Elsie picked up her tray and followed Amy's voice to the counter where they put their trays. When they went outside for recess, the first thing Elsie noticed was the cold bite of the wind. She wanted to get her hat out of her pocket, but she wanted to make sure she could swing with Amy and Krista more.

"Walk with Krista," Amy told her. "I'll go save swings for all of us."

Elsie let go of Amy's arm and reached for Krista. She heard Amy run off and hoped she would get to the swings in time to save three.

When they got to the swings, Krista put Elsie's hand on the swing. "Amy and I will be on either side of you."

When Elsie sat down, she pushed off with her foot and started pumping her legs. She loved going as high as she could.

Krista sat down on the swing on her right and said, "You know it's not really fair that they make you go to class with the rest of us."

"Why?" Elsie frowned.

Amy said, "Well you're blind. It is harder for you to do things like the rest of us. I mean, you had trouble playing dodgeball today."

"I don't think it's safe for you because our classmates don't look where they are going," Krista added. "If you hadn't stayed in the corner, you might have gotten trampled."

Elsie hated that a part of her agreed with Amy and Krista. She *was* afraid of being trampled when they played dodgeball, but she also wanted to do whatever the class was doing. "My mom and dad want me to do everything that the rest of you do," she said.

Amy *hmphed*. "I told my mom about your shirt being on inside-out yesterday, and she said that she doesn't understand why your parents make you go to public school instead of sending you to the school for the blind. Did you know there is a school for people like you?"

Elsie's face got warm. She thought about how ironic it was that she had been embarrassed because Amy had laughed at her, and then Amy's mom used her shirt being on inside-out as a reason she should go to the school for the blind.

"My parents told me that they talked about sending me there before I started kindergarten but decided not to because it's three hours away. If I went there, I would have to stay at school all week. My parents said they didn't want people they don't know raising me."

Krista sounded sad when she said, "My dad said he doesn't think you should be in class with the rest of us. He said if I were blind, he would send me to the school for the blind. He would be too worried about me getting made fun of if I stayed here."

Elsie felt anger begin to bubble in her chest. What made Amy and Krista's parents think they knew better than her own parents what would be best for her? "I have people here who can teach me how to do things," she said. "Laura showed me how to tell if my shirt is on inside-out, so that won't happen again."

"If you were with people like you, you wouldn't have been embarrassed because no one would've been able to see," Amy argued.

Elsie wondered why Amy thought that Elsie needed to be with people that were just like her, and what Amy's parents had told her about the school for the blind. "They have people who can see there. I think the teachers can see, and some of the students have a little vision."

Amy said, "Well it's good that the teachers can see, because they need to have people who can see to help the blind teachers and students."

"I understand that your parents didn't send you there when you were little because it's so far away, but what about now?" Krista asked. "You are older now. Wouldn't you want to go there and be with other blind kids?"

"I wouldn't want to go there now because I'm happy here."

"My family feels the same way Krista's does," Amy said. "They would send me to the school for the blind."

Elsie was silent for a minute. "I met some teachers from the school for the blind. A few years ago, one of them came here to give Mrs. Perry and my parents advice on how to help me. She didn't seem very nice."

Elsie heard Amy slow her swing. "Well maybe she was just having a bad day. Come on, Krista, I want to jump rope."

Krista slowed her swing and got off. Before she walked away with Amy, she said, "I'll see you later, Elsie."

As Elsie swung by herself, she thought about the school for the blind. *Were those teachers just having a difficult day? What would it be like to go to school with other blind kids?* Julie had introduced her to a few kids who were blind, but they were all older than her.

What would it be like to have other friends who were blind? Elsie did not think she would want another blind student in her school because then people might try and compare them. But it might be nice to have a friend her own age who was blind, if they went to different schools.

The only blind person she had ever met was Beth. Beth was one of Julie's students who was in high school, and sometimes came with Julie. Beth wanted to be a teacher like Julie, and Julie thought that Beth was a good role model for Elsie.

Elsie was not sure what she thought of Beth. On the one hand, she hated Beth because she made everything seem so easy. But she also wanted to be *like* Beth. Julie said that Beth always had good grades. She had told Elsie, "Beth makes the honor roll every semester. Don't you want to be like Beth?"

Elsie was more jealous of Beth's friends than her grades. Beth had lots of friends and was always talking about going to sleepovers and doing fun things together. Elsie had never been to a sleepover; another reason to be jealous of Beth.

She wondered how Beth made friends but did not want to ask because it seemed like everything was easy for Beth. She did not want Beth to know how hard it was for her to make friends. She wondered if Beth had ever done anything silly, like go to school with her shirt on inside-out. She doubted it because Beth was *perfect*.

Not only was Beth perfect, but she expected *Elsie* to be perfect as well. Elsie hated how condescending Beth sounded when she said, "I know you can do better than that, Miss Elsie." Elsie always wanted to answer back, "I'm glad that *you're* perfect, but I'm not and I don't know if I'll ever be. "To make things worse, even Elsie's parents thought Beth was perfect. After they saw her, they always told Elsie, "You'll have to work harder if you want to be like Beth."

Thinking about Beth reminded Elsie that Julie had talked about bringing Beth with her during spring break to help teach Elsie how to use her computer. She did not want Beth to come, because using a computer would be just one more thing that Beth could do better than Elsie. Elsie swung harder and passionately wished that there was *one* thing she could do better than Beth. Or, if there was not anything she could do better than Beth, she wanted to find something she could do as well as Beth.

Elsie decided to try and learn how to use her computer before spring break so that Julie would not ask Beth to come. Or if she did come, that she would be impressed with how well Elsie used her computer.

Chapter 7
Reading Upside-Down

When the class got inside, Elsie went to her desk and grabbed her history book. During history class, the class sat at the circle table and took turns reading. She hated reading aloud because she felt like she was the slowest reader in the class. Each classmate read at different speeds, and she found it hard to keep up with the faster readers. Everyone knew when she got lost, because the whole class had to stop and let Mrs. Perry help Elsie find her place in the book again.

Elsie did not mind reading aloud if she was the first one in the class to read. She could read her paragraph, and then listen while the others read. She had to pretend to keep reading along, because if she did not, then Mrs. Perry and Mrs. Conklin would say she was not paying attention. Once, she tried explaining to Mrs. Perry that she could pay better attention to the lesson if she was not worried about keeping up with the others; Mrs. Perry had told her that since the rest of the class had to read, Elsie did too.

When they had sat down, Mrs. Conklin asked, "Who wants to read first?" Elsie immediately raised her hand, but Mrs. Conklin said, "Elsie, you read first yesterday. I want someone else to read first today. Amy, you had your hand up. Please start where we left off yesterday."

Her heart sank. Reading after Amy was the worst. Amy was a speed reader, the fastest in the class. Elsie opened her book to where her bookmark was and realized that her book was upside-down. She also realized that Mrs. Perry was not in the room, as Mrs. Perry was the only other person in the classroom who could read braille, Elsie could pretend she did not know that her book was upside-down. Maybe, if she were lucky,

Mrs. Perry would not get back until history was over. Amy read her paragraph and Elsie pretended to follow along. In truth, it was easier to follow along when she just listened than it was when she tried to keep up with her reading. She slouched in her seat so Mrs. Conklin would not see her and call on her to read next. As minutes passed, Elsie had started to relax. History had to be almost over, and she had not been asked to read yet. Better yet, Mrs. Perry was not in the room, so nobody knew that her book was upside-down.

Elsie's relaxed mood vanished when Mrs. Conklin said, "Elsie, you have not read yet. Will you read now?"

"I'm sorry," Elsie said, "I can't find my place."

Mrs. Conklin sighed. "Alright, you can read when—"

Elsie gulped as she heard Mrs. Perry's shoes on the floor; her aide walked into the room right before Mrs. Conklin could call on someone else to read. Elsie knew that Mrs. Perry would be able to tell right away that her book was upside-down.

"Mrs. Perry, perfect timing. It is Elsie's turn to read, and she can't find her place."

Yes, perfect timing, Elsie thought as she waited for the inevitable.

"Where are you?" Mrs. Perry asked.

"We're starting the section on the Founding Fathers," said Mrs. Conklin. "There should be a heading that says, 'Founding Fathers.'"

Mrs. Perry walked over to Elsie's desk and squatted down so she could read the braille. Elsie moved her hand off the book so her teacher could read the braille. Her palms started sweating, and she wiped them on her pants.

"It would help if your book wasn't upside-down." Mrs. Perry took Elsie's hand and put it back on the book. "Can you read that? How did you not realize that this book was upside-down?"

Elsie heard the class laugh and wished she could sink through the floor. *Why, oh why did Mrs. Perry have to talk so loudly?* She knew if she told Mrs. Perry that Amy had been the first reader today and she could not keep up with Amy, Mrs. Perry would think it was an excuse. Elsie also realized that if she said that, Amy might think Elsie was blaming *her.* She decided that the best thing she could do right now was keep quiet as Mrs. Perry flipped the book right-side up and helped her find her place.

After history class was over, Elsie went to her reading class and prayed that Mrs. Perry would not say anything to her reading teacher, Mr. Dean. Thankfully, Mrs. Perry did not say anything, and Elsie dared to hope that Mrs. Perry and Mrs. Conklin had forgotten.

When the bell rang for the end of the day, Elsie went to her locker and grabbed her backpack. She put her books and homework folder in her backpack and wondered if Mrs. Perry would want to write a note to her parents about today. When she was about to zip up her backpack, Mrs. Perry walked over and told her, "Mrs. Conklin and I have decided that you will read an extra fifteen minutes tonight to make up for the time you wasted. Also, we will write a note to your parents telling them what you did today."

Elsie hung her head and said, "Okay."

As she listened to Mrs. Perry writing a note to her parents, she wondered if Mrs. Conklin wrote notes to the parents of her classmates when they did something bad. She thought about taking the note out of her backpack and throwing it away before she got home but knew that she would not have a chance. If she had been going home on the bus, maybe she could have taken it out of her backpack and left it on the seat. But she had to stay late today and would not ride on the bus.

Even as she thought about the idea, she knew that she could never do it. She did not like keeping things from her parents even when it was something that would get her in trouble. She would accept a night of no TV, or whatever punishment they thought was best.

Chapter 8
Street Crossings

Once her backpack was packed, Elsie waited in the classroom for Julie.

"Hi Elsie," Julie greeted her when she walked in. "Are you ready to go?"

"Yes. Are we stopping by the bakery today?"

"No not today. We're going to work on street crossings, and then end the day in your favorite store."

Elsie did not know whether to frown or cheer. She loved going to the bakery for an after-school snack, but she also loved ending the day at Pear Tree. The small consignment shop always had something interesting to look at.

When Julie parked the car downtown, Elsie got out and pulled on her hat and gloves. She hated working in the cold, and today it was freezing outside.

"Listen to the traffic," Julie instructed her. "Is it parallel or perpendicular to you?"

Elsie listened to the traffic and could tell the cars were running in front of her. Because it was the end of the day, there were lots of cars out. This made it easy to tell which way the traffic was running, but Elsie was tired, which made it hard to pay attention.

"They are perpendicular," she said.

"Do you think you should try to cross the street right now?"

Elsie was annoyed. She knew that Julie was trying to help her, but surely *everyone* knew that if you walked out into oncoming traffic, you would most likely end up as flat as a pancake.

"No," she answered.

"Then tell me when it is safe to cross the street."

Elsie listened to the traffic and wondered if it would ever change direction. It was not quite rush-hour, but close enough that traffic was heavy. As she waited for the traffic to change directions, the wind started blowing harder. *Of course, the wind would pick up now while I am waiting to cross the street,* she thought to herself. *How does this not bother Julie? I hate this! I am cold and hungry.*

She was so focused on her own thoughts that she almost missed the traffic changing directions, but finally she heard the shift in the noise.

"The traffic is running parallel. Can I cross now?" she asked Julie.

"Go ahead," Julie told her, so Elsie stepped off the curb and slowly made her way across the street.

"Pick up the pace!" Julie urged. "The traffic won't stay parallel forever!"

Elsie moved faster and made it across the street. They kept working on street crossings until Elsie thought she would freeze. She was thankful when they finally reached the Pear Tree.

When they walked inside the store, Elsie took off her hat and gloves and put them in the pockets of her coat. She sighed in relief, and then inhaled the distinct smell of the store. It smelled like old things, with a hint of cinnamon.

She was happy that they were inside, but her happiness turned to irritation when she realized that they had come in the back door. Julie loved coming in the back door because the path to the front of the store was never the same. The back of the store was for furniture, and Mrs. Philips, the store owner, was always getting new furniture and moving things around. Elsie wondered if Julie asked Mrs. Philips to move things on purpose.

"If you want to look at the stuffed animals, you have to make it to the front of the store without my help," Julie said.

Elsie almost groaned. It had been a long day, and she was tired. She did not want to work anymore. Besides, she still had a full night of homework ahead. Then, she thought about the stuffed animals. Maybe a little extra work would not be so bad if it meant she would get to see the stuffed animals.

She stood still and listened for a minute. She could hear people talking somewhere in the store. The voice she heard were closer to the front of the store, so she decided to follow them. Elsie swept her cane out in front of her, and it clanked against something. She reached out with her hand and found a chair. When she tried to walk around it, she found that she was stuck in between the chair and a table.

"Oh, great," she sighed. "Mrs. Philips got a new dining-room set that I'll have to work around."

Once she found her way around the table and chairs, she encountered a couch and a few other bits of furniture. She navigated around them as well and made it to the part of the shop that had shelves on both sides. She knew that once she found the shelves, there was an easy path to the front.

At the front of the store, she heard Mrs. Philips helping a customer check out. They were talking about the angel statue the customer purchased. Elsie cautiously reached to feel what was on the shelf to her left and felt some cups that she guessed were glass. She reached to feel what was on her right and found bowls. She walked forward and found the next set of shelves. This shelf had figurines.

Elsie was happy when she heard the customer leave the store. Julie had said that Elsie could not ask *her* for help, but she had not said anything about asking Mrs. Phillips.

"Hello Elsie," Mrs. Phillips called out. "How are you today, dear?"

"I'm good," Elsie answered. "It's nice to be in a warm store after being outside."

Mrs. Phillips laughed. "Are you looking for the stuffed animals?"

"Yes."

"You're doing a great job. They are on the next shelf on your left."

Elsie was thankful Mrs. Phillips had given her directions. She had not wanted to risk breaking something, but she also had not wanted to ask Mrs. Phillips and have Julie get mad at her. She walked to the next set of shelves, and touched the shelf on her left; there, she felt something soft and furry.

She liked all kinds of stuffed animals, but there was one animal on the shelf that grabbed her attention. It had the softest fur of all the stuffed animals in the shop. She picked it up and wondered what kind of animal it was. With her hands, she noticed it had two big, floppy ears, and a velvety nose. *It must be a bunny,* she decided.

Elsie slowly put the bunny back on the shelf with the other toys and said, "I'll have to tell Grandma about this bunny. Maybe she will buy it for me."

Standing beside her, Julie looked at the price tag. "It isn't expensive," she said. "I'll get it for you for doing such a good job today."

Elsie smiled. "Thank you."

When Julie had paid for the bunny, she handed the bag to Elsie. "I could tell you did your best today even though you were cold and hungry."

Elsie had not realized that Julie noticed that she was cold and hungry. It touched her to know that even when she did not say anything, Julie noticed what she was feeling. She tried not to complain because she knew that learning how to cross streets was important, but it was hard to stay focused when the wind stung your face and your stomach felt like it would tie itself in knots.

She felt proud that she had done something to make Julie proud of her. Julie did not often give compliments so when she did, Elsie knew she had done an excellent job. Elsie could count on one hand the number of times Julie had given her a reward for how well she had done. She knew if she was getting a reward, she had done especially well.

She had felt embarrassed and ashamed that she had pretended she did not know that her book was upside down. Getting a reward for doing well now took some of the shame away. She thought that having her bunny would help her remember what she could do if she really tried. She promised herself that she would try to not worry so much about what other people thought of her.

Chapter 9
Differing Opinions

When Julie dropped her off at home, Elsie's dad was there to meet them.

"Hi Julie," he said. "How did she do today?"

"She did very well today. We practiced street crossings and ended the day at her favorite store."

Dad put his arm around Elsie. "I bet she loved that."

"Yes, she did. I bought her a stuffed animal because she did so well today."

Dad squeezed her shoulder and said, "She is spoiled."

Julie laughed and got back in the car. "I'll see you on Thursday, Elsie."

"See you Thursday," Elsie called.

Once they were in the house, Dad asked Elsie, "How was your day?"

Elsie thought for a moment. She did not want to say that she had a dreadful day, but it was not a good day either. Mostly, she wished that she could forget about trying to read upside-down, but she knew Dad would want to talk about it once he read the note. She shrugged and handed him her backpack.

"It was okay, I guess."

She heard him unzip her backpack, and quickly left to put her new bunny in her room. When she walked back into the kitchen, she sniffed. She had not noticed it before, but now she could smell something cooking.

"What's for dinner?" she asked.

Elsie heard her dad fold a piece of paper and guessed he had read the note.

"Taco salad," he said. Inside her head, Elsie groaned. She could tell by his voice that he was not happy. She sat down at the table and prepared for a lecture.

"Elsie, why did you pretend you didn't know your book was upside-down?"

"Because I hate reading out loud," she said. "I'm sure that I'm the slowest reader in the class."

"Do you think you're the only one who hates reading out loud?" he asked. "Think about the kids in your special education reading class. They are probably like you and do not mind reading aloud when they are in a room full of kids who struggle to read. But how do you think they feel when they go back to their classrooms and must read aloud in front of kids who probably read just as fast, as if not faster, than Amy?"

Elsie thought about that for a second. She had not ever thought about how the other kids in her reading class felt when they were in their regular classrooms. Maybe they hated reading aloud as much as she did. At least in her reading class, everyone read below their grade level.

"I hadn't thought about that. But it is more than just not liking it. I have a tough time focusing when I am trying to keep up with the rest of the class. I always have to go back and read the chapter again because I can't keep up *and* focus on the lesson."

Her dad was silent for a second. "Hmm. Have you talked to Mrs. Perry about this?"

Elsie sighed. "I've tried to talk to her, but she thinks I'm just making excuses!"

"Well, I can understand why she might think that when you pretend you don't know your book is upside-down."

"I tried talking to her about it before today!" Elsie exclaimed.

"Calm down," Dad said gently. "I understand why you are frustrated. What do you think will help you?"

"It's easier for me when I can be the first to read. Then I can try to keep up, but mostly focus on paying attention to the lesson."

Dad thought about that for a minute. Finally, he sighed and said, "Alright. I'll write a note to Mrs. Perry and Mrs. Conklin and ask if we can try having you read first for a couple weeks to see how that goes."

"Thanks, Dad," Elsie said.

You have to promise that you won't pretend your book is upside-down again."

"I promise."

*

When Elsie's mom got home from work, she walked into the kitchen and kissed Elsie on the top of her head. "How was your day?" she asked.

Before Elsie could think of what to say, Dad said, "Elsie pretended that she didn't know her history book was upside-down today."

"Elsie!" Mom exclaimed. "Why would you do that?"

Elsie explained again about how much she hated to read aloud, and how hard it was to focus on the lesson when she had to try to keep up with the rest of the class.

Dad followed up, saying, "I told Elsie I would write a note to Mrs. Perry and Mrs. Conklin asking if she could read first, *if* she promised to not pretend, she doesn't know when her book is upside-down."

Mom ruffled Elsie's hair and said, "That sounds fair. You can't avoid reading out loud, but maybe we can make it easier to focus."

"I won't do it again," Elsie promised.

Dad said, "Supper is ready, and you've finished your extra reading assignment. You can write about what you read after supper."

After they all sat down to eat, Elsie said, "Today at recess Amy and Krista let me swing with them. They acted like they wanted to hang out, but then Amy asked when I was going to the school for the blind. Amy's mom told her that I was going to go there. Krista said that her dad said that he would make her go to the school for the blind if she was blind."

"Mommy, what is the school for the blind?" Blake asked with a mouth full of taco salad.

"Blake, don't talk with food in your mouth," Mom scolded. "The school for the blind is a special school that is just for blind kids."

Elsie heard her dad crunch a few corn chips. When he swallowed, he said, "Lots of people assume that, because you are blind, we are going to send you to the school for the blind. They think it would be better for you to be in a school with kids who are just like you, and teachers who are trained to help you."

Elsie took a bite of her taco salad and thought about what her dad said. "I know you didn't send me there when I was little because you felt like other people would be raising me, but what about now? Do you think I should go there?"

"If Elsie went away to school, I would be the only kid in the house," Blake interrupted.

Mom drank from her glass and added, "You would miss your sister if she went away to school. Who would play with you?"

Everyone was quiet, and Elsie wondered if her pretending with her book this afternoon made them think she should go to the school for the blind.

Finally, her dad said, "Your mom and I have talked about it, and we aren't crazy about the idea of you being away from home all week, but you might get a better education if you had teachers specially trained to help you."

"Julie is trained to help me," Elsie argued.

Dad took a drink and said, "You only see Julie twice a week."

"We want you to have friends here." Mom said. "If you go to the school for the blind, your friends would be scattered all over Missouri."

"Elsie doesn't have friends," Blake said.

"Shut up, Blake!" Elsie snapped. Then to her parents she said, "You always told me it was my choice whether I went there or not."

Mom took a drink. "Don't tell your brother to shut up. And it is still your choice. We won't send you there unless you want to go."

Her dad went to get a second helping of taco salad. "Krista's dad probably thinks that it isn't safe for you to go to public school. You know from firsthand experience that kids can be mean. He probably thinks that at the school for the blind, no one would make fun of you."

Elsie gulped the rest of her tea. "Do you think that's true?"

Dad took a bite of taco salad and said, "Kids are kids. It does not matter if you have a disability or not. They'll find something to tease you about."

"Can I talk about my day at Linda's now?" Blake whined.

Mom stood up and picked up Elsie's plate and cup, then carried them to the sink and turned on the water. "Yes, Blake. We're sorry you didn't get a chance to tell us about your day during dinner."

Elsie only half-paid attention to her brother. Her thoughts were still on the school for the blind. She hated that people who did not know her assumed the school would be the best place for her.

When it was bedtime, her dad came in to tuck her in. "Don't worry about what Amy and Krista say," he told her. "Everyone has an opinion on everything, so let it roll off you like water rolls off a duck's feathers."

Elsie snuggled under the covers. "It is hard to ignore them, but I'll try."

Her dad put her teddy bear and new bunny under the covers before pulling them up over Elsie.

"Let's have a better day tomorrow, sissy. I know you can do better. Your little brother looks up to you, and you are an example for him. I know he gets on your nerves, but one day he is going to say, 'If my sissy can do it, I can do it.'"

"Okay," she promised. "I'll do better."

Dad kissed the top of her head "I love you sis. See you tomorrow."

Elsie's mom came in and said "Goodnight. See you in the morning."

Elsie said her prayers, held her new stuffed bunny tight, and fell fast asleep.

Chapter 10

Sleepover and a First Crush

The next morning, Elsie tried to think positively about the day ahead. Today was Wednesday, her favorite day of the week, because in the evening Grandma Sally would come pick her up and take her to church for choir practice and midweek classes. She loved choir practice because she loved to sing. Elsie had always loved music, and she loved sharing her talent with the congregation.

Midweek class was a lot like Sunday School, in that they learned about different Bible stories. Elsie was quite sure she knew all the popular Bible stories by heart, but she always found something new to think about. Elsie thought that the best thing about midweek was that they got snacks at the end, and you only got snacks in Sunday School on special occasions. Elsie prayed the school day would fly by so she could get to her favorite part of the week.

When she got to school, Mrs. Lester took Elsie into the gym and seated her by Amy and Krista. Minutes passed, and the other two girls did not even say hello to her; Elsie started to wonder if she was invisible. Amy and Krista were so absorbed in their conversation that it seemed they had not even noticed she was sitting by them.

"You can come home with me after school on Friday and we can play with Princess," Amy was telling Krista. "My grandma got her some bows to put on her collar, and she has a few sweaters."

Krista squealed and clapped her hands. "That sounds like fun! I cannot wait to see Princess! What else will we do?"

"My dad said that we could order pizza and watch a movie, and maybe on Saturday morning we can take Princess to the pet store and give her a bath."

"That sounds like fun," Krista said. "I can bring my camera and we can take pictures of her taking a bath!"

"That would be great," Amy agreed. "We can post the pictures on Facebook and Instagram!"

Elsie was friends with Amy and Krista on Facebook and had scrolled past some of Amy's posts about Princess. Amy never posted captions with her pictures, but Elsie's phone tried to describe the picture. It would say things like "picture of one person and dog." Sometimes Elsie would read the comments on Amy's posts to see what was so special about the picture.

She wished she could meet Princess. She loved dogs, and she wished she could pet Princess, so she had a better idea of what Amy's pictures looked like. A sleepover would be a fun time to meet Princess. Elsie wondered if Amy would ever invite her to a sleepover.

"I love puppies," she said. "Do you think I could see Princess some time?"

There was a moment of silence. "Oh . . . Well, maybe I can bring her to school for show-and-tell some time," Amy said.

Elsie felt awkward. She had been trying to hint that she would like an invitation to their sleepover. *Had Amy not understood what she meant, or did she not want to invite Elsie?* Elsie was silent as she listened to Amy and Krista talk about what they would dress Princess in after her bath. She *really* wanted to help Amy and Krista give Princess a bath, so she decided to try again.

"I would love to have a sleepover with you sometime," she said hopefully.

Amy touched Elsie's arm. "I'm sorry, but I can only have one person at my house at a time."

Elsie spent the morning wondering if there was something she could do to make Amy and Krista want to be her friends. *Did she need to post more on social media? Did she need nicer clothes?* She did not know much about Krista, but she knew that Amy's family was rich, and she got everything she wanted.

A few years ago, Amy had gone to the American Girl Doll Store and gotten a real American Girl doll for Christmas. Elsie had been jealous of Amy because she had only gotten one of the Our Generation dolls from Target. She had felt embarrassed when they both brought their dolls to show-and-tell because all the girls liked Amy's doll better. Elsie had to admit that even she liked Amy's doll better. Amy told the class about eating in the cafe and how they had little chairs for the dolls to sit in. Amy and her doll even had matching outfits.

Someone sat down beside Elsie, pulling her from her thoughts. She felt a light tap on her shoulder and turned to face the newcomer.

"Hi, I'm Tanner," a boy's voice said.

Elsie smiled. "Hi. I am Elsie. We are in the same class, aren't we?"

"Yes. I wanted to tell you that I think it's cool that your phone talks to you."

"Thanks. It is nice to be able to text and be on social media like everyone else. I was using my mom's old iPod, but it finally stopped working a few weeks before Christmas."

"It's lucky that it stopped working a few weeks before Christmas when everything is on sale," Tanner joked.

Elsie laughed. "Yeah, it was kind of lucky. Mom and Dad decided I was responsible enough to have a phone. When I asked if I could have a Facebook account, they said I could, but I had to give them the password so they could see what I was doing."

"That's cool. Hey, I'll add you on Facebook."

Elsie felt her heart skip a beat. A boy was going to add her on Facebook! And she had not asked him to add her; he *wanted* to add her!

Tanner asked, "How does your phone talk to you? My phone doesn't talk to me."

"It might talk to you. A lot of phones have voices in them now. You just have to know how to turn the voice on."

"I'm going to try to see if my phone has a voice and turn it on."

"Be careful," Elsie warned. "Once you turn on the voice, it changes the way you use your phone. It might be hard for you to turn off the voice once you've turned it on."

"I probably shouldn't turn it on then. I am using my big sister's old phone, and she might kill me if I broke it."

Elsie laughed. "I would probably be mad too if my little brother borrowed something from me and then broke it."

Tanner laughed too. "I still want to see if my phone has a voice. How do I find it?"

"It depends on what kind of phone you have. If you have an iPhone, you go into 'settings' and then into 'accessibility' and you will find it. The program is called Voiceover. I don't know about other types of phones."

They were silent for a minute before Tanner asked, "What kind of music do you like?"

"I like country and Christian pop," Elsie said.

"I like country as well. My favorite singer is Eric Church."

"I like him too. I'm not sure who my favorite is though."

When the bell rang, Mrs. Lester had to struggle to get everyone's attention.

"Boys and girls! you know the rules: when the bell rings, you stop talking!" But it still took a few minutes for everyone to stop talking and for Mrs. Lester to dismiss each grade.

Finally, Mrs. Lester said, "Fifth grade, you may now walk to your classrooms."

Tanner leaned toward her and whispered, "Can I walk with you to class?"

Elsie smiled. "Sure, I would love that."

When they got to class, Tanner said goodbye to Elsie at her desk and walked away. Elsie took her books out of her backpack and gave her homework folder to Mrs. Perry.

"Here is last night's homework."

"Thank you," said Mrs. Perry. "Did I see you walk into the classroom with Tanner?"

"Yes. He came and sat by me; we talked about my new phone and what kind of music we like. We both like country music."

"Tanner is a nice boy."

"I would like to talk to him more," Elsie smiled.

As she started her morning work, Elsie thought about how weird life was. Just last night she was looking at stuffed animals, and now today she had her first crush.

Chapter 11

Art Class

When everyone had finished their morning work, it was time for math. Some of the class left the room to go to Mrs. Dowling's room. Mrs. Dowling taught the kids that could do more advanced math, and Mrs. Conklin taught the kids that needed a little more help.

Elsie was thankful that both Amy and Krista were in the advanced class. She did not want them to know how much she struggled with math. Elsie did not know what Mrs. Dowling's class was working on, but her class had just started working with fractions. Elsie kind of enjoyed fractions because her book had cool pictures that she could feel, and each fraction had different textures. One picture that was supposed to look like a piece of pie had bumps on all the pieces of the pie, and smooth lines to show where they were divided.

The picture of a pie in her math book made her think of a book she read when she was little called *Bumpy Rolls Away*. The book was about a ball that gets thrown too far, and the adventures it has before finding its way back home. Elsie loved it because it was one of the few braille books that had pictures. The ball in the book was just a circle with bumps inside it. The bumps in the circle made Elsie think that maybe the ball was supposed to be a basketball because basketballs had bumps on them. If the picture in her math book did not have the dividing lines on it, it would look just like Bumpy.

It was hard to stay focused after Elsie realized that the fractions in her textbook looked like Bumpy the Ball divided into fourths. She could not stop imagining all the ways Bumpy could get divided into fourths.

Elsie was happy when math was over, but she groaned inwardly when she remembered that she had art class next.

Elsie wanted to do everything her classmates did, but art was *boring*. She had trouble drawing shapes. Elsie knew that to draw a square you went down and over then back up and over. But few times she tried to draw a square with puffy paint, her squares never looked like the ones Mrs. Perry drew. Because Elsie had trouble drawing shapes, Mrs. Perry made the outline of whatever they were working on with Wikki Stix. That way, Elsie did not have to worry about her pictures looking like whatever they were working on; she could just color in the lines.

Once everyone was seated in the art classroom, Mr. Jones clapped his hands for silence. "Alright, it's a new year, and we are starting a new project." He did a drumroll on the desk before he continued speaking. "We're starting self-portraits! I want two people from each table to come up to the front and get paper and a box of markers for your table."

The room filled with chatter as kids from each of the round tables went to get paper and markers, and Mr. Jones clapped his hands again. "I do not want to hear talking. You can't focus on your art if you are talking to your friends."

Everyone stopped talking, and soon Elsie heard markers scraping across paper as the class started working on their pictures.

Mr. Jones walked over to Elsie and said, "I asked Mrs. Perry to make the outline of a person with Wikki Stix so you can color it. You should use brown for your hair and blue for your eyes."

Elsie wondered if Mr. Jones thought she did not know what color her hair and eyes were. Even though she could not look in a mirror, she knew what she looked like. When she was younger, she had asked her mom and dad, and they told her that she had light brown hair and blue eyes.

"I brought you your scented markers so you can tell what color you're using," Mr. Jones said.

Elsie wondered why he thought she could tell what color the marker was by the scent. She did not associate color with scents; she associated each color with something in her life. For example, if someone said something was black, she thought of thunder because she loved thunderstorms, and people said that a lot of times during a thunderstorm the sky was black. Green was confusing because there were so many variations of green. She knew that green was used for Christmas and Easter, but the Easter green was a lighter green. She thought of grass for the light green and peppermint for the dark green.

Elsie wondered if it was weird that she never thought of her hair or eyes when someone talked about brown or blue. If someone said something was brown, she thought of chocolate. If someone said something was blue, she either thought of cold or blueberries. She was not sure why blue made her think of cold, but it did.

Because the markers were scented with things that most sighted people associated with a color, Elsie had trouble figuring out what each color was supposed to smell like. She knew the markers had their scents on their labels, but she could not read the label. The only one she knew for sure was the green marker, because it smelled like peppermint. Elsie loved the scent of peppermint, and when she realized there was a peppermint marker, she had asked what color it was.

Mr. Jones set the paper and box of markers in front of her and walked away. Elsie traced her fingers over the outline of a person and thought about where to start. It would be best to start with her hair and eyes, she decided. But as she pulled her box of markers closer, she realized she had a problem: she did not know what the brown marker was supposed to smell like. She assumed that the brown would smell like chocolate, so she started to search for a chocolate-scented marker.

She picked up each marker and sniffed it but could not find any that smelled like chocolate. Elsie decided that if the brown marker was supposed to smell like chocolate, the factory had not done a respectable job with the scent.

Elsie was embarrassed that she could not find the brown marker. The scented markers were supposed to help her know what color each marker was, but she could not tell what most of the scents were. *How could she tell what color a marker was if she could not even tell what it was supposed to smell like?*

She decided to work on her shirt first. She wanted to draw her favorite fuzzy sweater but did not know how to draw the fuzz. She grabbed the green marker and started making little circles that were supposed to be the fuzz on her sweater. While she colored, she thought about Tanner. She liked that he came over to her by himself, without being asked by one of the teachers. She hoped that he would talk to her again and maybe, by the end of the year, he would be her boyfriend.

She imagined the two of them dancing at the end-of-school dance. She thought about the dress she would wear, and what songs they would play. After a while, she realized she had gotten so caught up in the daydream that she had stopped drawing circles and was just coloring in the outline. She touched the picture and could tell that she had colored so much in one place, the marker had bled through the paper.

Elsie thought again about how much she hated art. She could not color the shirt any more without ruining it, and she did not know what to work on next because she could not tell what color any of the other markers were supposed to be.

Finally, she decided to color the pants green as well. That would save her from picking a color that did not match green, or accidentally coloring her hair pink, or something crazy like that. The class would surely laugh at her if she accidentally colored her hair pink.

She spent the rest of class coloring the pants and wondering if Tanner would talk to her again. When Mr. Jones told the class it was time to stop working, Elsie put the green marker away and sighed with relief.

"One person from each table can put away the markers, and I will come collect your pictures and write your names on the back of them. I love to see what everyone has accomplished."

As Elsie listened, Mr. Jones commented on each person's drawing. He gave everyone helpful tips and suggestions on how to make their art better. She wondered what he would say about *her* drawing.

When he got to her, he picked up her picture and looked at it for a minute.

"You did a good job today, Elsie," he finally said. "You must love the color green, because you made your shirt and pants green."

It was easier for her to do a decent job because all she had to do was color in the lines. Everyone else had to draw themselves. But even though it was easier for her, Elsie knew she had not done an excellent job, not really. She had used green on both the shirt and pants when she knew she should have used two distinct colors, and she had colored so much in one spot that the marker bled through the paper.

Elsie wondered why Mr. Jones had lied and told her she had done a respectable job when she knew she had not.

*

That day at lunch, Tanner sat by Elsie. Elsie was glad that he sat by her, and she wanted to talk to him, but she did not quite know what to say. Tanner was not easy to talk to. He chewed with his mouth open and seemed to be eating fast.

"The food is really good today." She decided that talking about the food would be a good topic of conversation.

Tanner swallowed and said, "Yeah, it's really good. I love corndogs and tater-tots."

She did not know what to say after that, and Tanner seemed to be more interested in his food than in talking to her. She listened to him smack his lips and wondered if she should ask him to eat with his mouth closed. Elsie remembered when she used to eat with her mouth open. Her mom had taught her that eating with your mouth open was bad manners; she had chewed with her mouth open every time Elsie did, and Elsie quickly learned that the sound was annoying and disgusting. She had not chewed with her mouth open since then.

Elsie was thankful when Dillon said, "That food isn't going to run away from you. Why are you eating so fast?"

She felt bad for Tanner; she knew what it felt like to be embarrassed in front of the class.

"I have to hurry because I want to see if there are any tater-tots left," Tanner said.

Elsie had eaten all she wanted and still had a few tater-tots left. She did not know if it was allowed, but she decided to give Tanner her leftover tater-tots anyway. She pushed her tray toward him and said, "You can have my leftover tater-tots."

"Are you sure you don't want any more?"

"Yes, I'm sure."

Amy said, "You're only giving him your tater-tots because you don't want to dump them in the trash can. You've been making sure you eat everything on your plate since that day you accidentally dumped green beans on the floor and Mrs. Lester yelled at you to be more careful."

"I gave him my tater-tots because I'm full, and he is still hungry," Elsie said.

Amy snorted. "Whatever. We all got the same amount of food he did, and you don't see anyone else scarfing their food down like a pig so they can go get more."

Elsie heard Tanner gulp. "I didn't get to school in time to eat breakfast. My mom's car wouldn't start, and we had to wait for her friend to give us a ride."

Dillon said, "Why didn't you just eat something at home?"

Elsie wondered if the other kids did not realize that the school breakfast was for kids who did not have enough to eat at home. She knew about it because her church donated backpacks and food for the "buddy pack" program. She had overheard one of the women say, "I did not buy any breakfast food because I did not know what to buy. Most of the nonperishable breakfast food is junk, and I do not want to support unhealthy eating habits. At least those poor kids get a healthy breakfast at school during the week."

The more Elsie thought about Tanner not getting to eat breakfast, the more she felt sorry for him. Elsie could not stand being hungry. Her stomach felt like it would eat itself, and it made her *so* angry. Her mom joked that she had "hanger" issues. As she thought about how she felt when she was hungry, she wondered how Tanner had gotten through morning classes. Elsie was glad she had given him her tater-tots. Yes, it was nice to not have to dump them in the trash, but it made her happy to know that Tanner's stomach would not feel like it would eat itself now.

Elsie wondered if Tanner felt embarrassed or ashamed because he did not answer Dillon's question. She heard Tanner's chair scrape the floor, and then he asked her, "Would you like me to take your tray for you?"

Elsie thought for a second. Mrs. Perry liked her to do as much as she could for herself. Normally, she would walk with Amy or Krista to put her own tray away. But surely it would not hurt to let Tanner do it since he had offered.

"That would be nice," she said. "Thank you."

Tanner took both of their trays to the dish pit. She heard the "clink" as he dropped their silverware into the bin. When he got back, he asked, "Can I swing with you at recess?"

"I'd like that," she said.

When their class was dismissed from the cafeteria, Elsie took Tanner's arm, and he walked her to the swings. She sat down and started pumping her legs, and heard Tanner start to swing beside her.

"I've seen you swinging a lot," he said. "Why do you like it so much?"

"I like to pretend that the swing can take me anywhere I want to go."

"I've never flown before, but I imagine that swinging feels a bit like flying."

"My family flew to Florida a few years ago," Elsie told him. "Swinging does feel a bit like flying, but flying is more fun. It's so exciting when the plane takes off and lands."

"You're lucky," Tanner said. "My family has never taken a vacation."

Elsie did not know what to say after that. As she swung, she thought about Tanner saying she was lucky. She knew that what Tanner called "lucky," others called "blessed." Elsie started to wonder if she was blessed. She would not call her blindness lucky or a blessing. It made her life harder in many ways. But she realized that she was blessed in other ways. She always had enough to eat, and a pantry full of her favorite snacks. She had a nice house that was safe and warm, and a family who loved her.

She wondered why she was so blessed, and other people were not. Elsie wished she had not said anything about her trip to Florida. *Would Tanner think she was bragging that she got to go on a nice vacation?* She hated when Amy bragged about something new, she got, or a vacation trip. Elsie did not want Tanner to think she was bragging, so she decided to explain how she had gotten to go to Florida.

"I got to go to Florida because the Dream Factory paid for it," Elsie told him as they kept swinging.

"What's the Dream Factory?"

"The Dream Factory is an organization that helps make the dreams of kids with illnesses come true. I am not sick, but I guess my blindness counts. One of my dad's friends gave them my name."

"That's cool that they paid for your trip," Tanner said. "When my mom, sister, and I go to my grandparents' house they always pay for our gas."

Elsie realized that this was another way she was blessed. All her family lived close by, and she could see them every week. "Do you get to go see them often?" she asked him.

"We see them for Christmas break and during the summer. Mom says we might go to see them during spring break this year."

"So did you go see them this Christmas?"

"Yes, and I had to help my grandpa get the Christmas tree loaded in the truck after my grandma, mom, and sister chose the biggest one on the lot."

Elsie realized that this was a way that Tanner was blessed. "That's cool," she said. "I have asked my parents so many times fora a real tree at Christmas, but Mom says they make her sneeze. I think she just does not want to clean up the pine needles that fall off."

Tanner laughed. "If you can't see, and you haven't ever had a real tree, how do you know about the pine needles falling off?"

"My grandma told me about having a real tree when she was a little girl."

"My grandparents always say that my sister and I need to know what things were like in the good old days."

Elsie laughed. "They sound like Grandma Sally. She is always saying, 'Things aren't like they were when I was little.'" Elsie and Tanner both laughed at that, and she was sad when the whistle blew for the end of recess.

"Will you swing with me again sometime?" Elsie asked as she stopped her swing, got off, and took Tanner's arm.

"Sure," he agreed. "I am going to play ball with my friends tomorrow, but I will swing with you again some time. We can talk in the morning though if you want."

"I'd like that," Elsie said.

As he walked her to line up with their class, Tanner said, "Thanks for letting me join you. I have never swung before. It was fun doing something new."

Elsie smiled. "I am glad you joined me. I do not really like swinging alone."

"If I see you swinging alone again, I'll come join you," he promised.

It made Elsie feel good that someone wanted to spend time with her. As she walked into the classroom, she felt like she was walking on air.

Chapter 12
Sighted Guide

After history class, Elsie went to Mr. Dean's room for English. She hated being the only one to leave the class for English, because everyone knew that if you went to Mr. Dean's room, you needed extra help. When she got to his classroom, Mr. Dean was not there yet, and the other students were waiting outside.

Mika said, "He's not here, and we don't know where he is."

Amber wondered, "Should we go back to our classrooms?"

Elsie thought about it for a second. "No, I think we should wait here. If he's not going to be here today, someone will tell us."

Not long after, Elsie heard footsteps. Two people walked down the hall toward them.

"Class, we have a new student joining us," Mr. Dean said. "This is Shaylyn. Her family just moved here. She has spent the past few days taking tests. I expect you all to make her feel welcome. Shaylyn," he continued, "is there anyone you know in this class?"

"Elsie and I are on the same bus," she said. "Can I sit by her?"

Mr. Dean sounded pleased when he said, "That would be fine. I'm sure Elsie would be delighted to have you sit by her." After everyone walked into the classroom, he pulled an empty desk closer to Elsie's. "Shaylyn, you can sit here. It is a good thing we just started a new book. We are reading *Out of My Mind* by Sharon M. Draper. Would someone like to tell Shaylyn what the book is about?"

Elsie raised her hand, but Mr. Dean called on Amber.

"The book is about a girl named Melody who is in fifth grade like us. She has…" There was silence while Amber tried to remember the name of Melody's condition.

"Can anyone else remember?" Mr. Dean asked. Elsie raised her hand again, and he said, "Elsie, what is the name of Melody's condition?"

"She has cerebral palsy," Elsie answered.

"Very good. I do not want to give too much away before Shaylyn reads chapters one and two. Shaylyn, I am going to let you listen to the first two chapters on the iPad today during class. If you finish them before we start reading chapter three, you can read with us."

Elsie thought Shaylyn was lucky. Mr. Dean rarely let anyone listen to a book on the iPad. He always said that they were in this class to work on their reading skills.

When Shaylyn finished listening to the first two chapters, the class was still discussing chapter two.

"Shaylyn," Mr. Dean said, "would you like to tell us what you think about the first two chapters?"

"Oh. Um. Well. I think it would be hard to not be able to talk or move. Melody talks about how there are things she wants to tell her parents, but she cannot. I would hate not being able to tell my parents what kind of music I like or that I love them. Also, it is cool the way she can smell music."

Mr. Dean said, "The book has not told us yet, but that is called synesthesia. Synesthesia is when you experience one of your senses through another. The book gives us a good example when it talks about Melody smelling and tasting lemons when she hears country music and smelling dirt when she listens to jazz."

"I agree with Shaylyn that synesthesia is cool, but it must have been frustrating not being able to tell her parents what she was experiencing." Mika said.

"Mika, please remember to raise your hand when you have something to say."

"Sorry," he mumbled.

"Does anyone else have anything to say about chapter two?" Mr. Dean asked. No one said anything, so he told Shaylyn, "Here is a copy of the book for you to borrow. Will you start reading chapter three aloud?"

While Elsie opened her book to her bookmark, she could hear Shaylyn flipping through her book to get to chapter three. Elsie did not mind being first to read in this class. Since everyone had trouble reading, she was not embarrassed to be a slow reader.

When Shaylyn started to read, Elsie could tell that she hated reading aloud. She could not see her face, but she could tell Shaylyn was about to cry because of the quiver in her voice. Elsie had no trouble keeping up with Shaylyn, and when Mr. Dean asked who wanted to read next, Elsie volunteered to read.

*

When the end-of-day bell rang, Elsie put her books and homework folder in her backpack and walked with Mrs. Perry to the bus stop. After they got there, Shaylyn walked up to Elsie and said, "I'm glad you are in my reading class, Elsie. Can I sit with you on the bus again?"

Mrs. Perry said, "Will you help Elsie get on the bus? I have some things I need to work on before I leave."

Shaylyn hesitated for a second. "Sure, but I don't know how to help her."

"Let her take your elbow and walk with you." Mrs. Perry demonstrated by gently bumping Elsie with her elbow. Elsie knew that this was her cue to hold on to Mrs. Perry's arm; they developed this signal when they first started working together.

"If you're going through a narrow space, put your arm behind you." Mrs. Perry moved her arm behind her back and Elsie stepped behind her. "When you're going up or down steps, tell Elsie you are at the steps, and then put her hand on the rail."

"Yes, I can do that," Shaylyn said.

"Then I will see you girls tomorrow." Elsie could hear Mrs. Perry's footsteps as she walked away. She was glad that Shaylyn was able to help her. There were always several buses parked outside the school loading kids. Elsie was afraid that if she went out there alone, she would get on the wrong bus.

"Okay, I'm right in front of you," Shaylyn said after their bus number was announced. Elsie reached forward but could not find her. Then she felt Shaylyn lightly tap her with her elbow. "Sorry, I forgot."

Elsie could tell that Shaylyn was nervous. She took the other girl's elbow, and they walked out to the bus together. Once they reached the bus steps, Shaylyn stopped and said, "So I just put your hand on the rail?"

"Yes," Elsie said. Shaylyn put Elsie's hand on the rail, and she walked up the bus steps. She walked to her normal seat behind the driver and scooted over so Shaylyn could sit beside her.

"That wasn't hard," Shaylyn said. "Maybe I could help you again sometime."

"Sure. I bet Mrs. Perry would love it if you and I walked out to the bus together from now on."

"You won't be on the bus tomorrow, right?" Shaylyn asked.

"Right," Elsie agreed. "I have to work with Julie."

"I saw you at recess today with a boy who is in your class."

"That's Tanner," Elsie smiled. "I want him to be my boyfriend."

"That's cool. The first two days of school, I saw you with those two prissy girls from your class."

"Amy and Krista," Elsie said. "What makes you think they're prissy?"

"I'm sorry, it's just the way they dress and act. I am sorry if I made you mad. I just wanted to ask if I could play with you some time? Now that I know how to help you, I could meet you outside and walk with you to the swings, or if you want, you could playhouse with me and a few girls from my class."

"You didn't make me mad," Elsie said. "Amy can sometimes be prissy, but they are both nice. I would like to play with you sometime."

Shaylyn bounced a little in the seat. "It will be nice to have someone else to play with at recess. I play with Hannah and Zoe most days, but all they want to do is hang out in the playhouse. We don't actually playhouse, we just stand in there and talk."

"It has been cold the past few days. They would do something else if it were warmer."

"Maybe. It is nice in the playhouse. It blocks us from the wind, and when we huddle together it's a bit warmer."

"That sounds cozy. I would like to join you on the next windy day," Elsie said.

Shaylyn touched Elsie's arm and said, "Sure, I'd love to have you join us."

"Hannah and Zoe won't mind?"

"No. They are curious about you, but they are afraid to talk to you. When I told them that I sat by you on the bus, they thought that was cool."

Elsie smiled. "I like sitting with you."

The bus came to a stop, and Elsie felt Shaylyn reach under the seat for her backpack. Elsie heard a "swish" as Shaylyn slid her backpack on over her winter coat. Before she left, she touched Elsie's arm again and said, "I am glad I have someone to sit with on the bus, and I am glad you are in the special reading class with me. It was scary going there for the first time."

Elsie smiled. It made her feel good to know that her being there made Shaylyn feel more comfortable.

Chapter 13
Choir Practice

Grandma Sally arrived to take Elsie to choir practice and midweek at their family church just as she was finishing her dinner.

"You need to hurry or we're going to be late," she said.

Elsie crammed the last bite of her garlic bread in her mouth and drank the rest of her tea. "I'm ready."

When they got in the car, Grandma Sally started the engine and then asked, "Why did you pretend you didn't know that your book was upside-down at school?"

Elsie rested her head on the back of the seat and said, "How do you know about that?"

"Your mom told me," Grandma Sally said. "You said that you were going to do better."

Elsie felt her shoulders tense up. She was annoyed that Grandma Sally was mentioning this when she had already talked with her parents about it. "I don't like reading after Amy because she's the fastest reader in the class."

Her grandma squeezed her arm and said, "It doesn't matter if you like reading after Amy or not. You need to do what the teachers tell you to do." Grandma Sally turned on her blinker. "I'm sure it's embarrassing to read after someone who is a fast reader, but you have to be like a duck and let it roll off of you."

Elsie felt the car turn and heard Grandma Sally turn off the blinker. She sighed. Her grandma often told her that she had to let things roll off her like water rolls off a duck's feathers. When she was little and something had upset her, her grandma had always told her to be a duck. When Grandma Sally said this, she often made funny quacking sounds that always made Elsie laugh. She did not think she would ever be a duck, but she did not want to tell her grandma that.

When they got to church, Grandma sat her on the steps by the other kids. A lot of the kids in choir were younger than she was. There were a few kids her age, but most of the kids her age had some sort of sports practice.

One of the few kids in choir that was her age was Abby. Abby sometimes sat by her, depending on who else was in choir that night. Abby never sat with her during Sunday school because her best friend, Amanda, was always there. Abby and Amanda did everything together: they were in Girl Scouts together, they had sleepovers at each other's houses, and they both went to the Lutheran school. The only thing that they did not do together was sports. Amanda played basketball and had to be at practice on Wednesday. Because Amanda was not here tonight, Abby sat by Elsie. Abby's twin Eli was there too, but he sat with a few of the younger boys.

Abby said, "How is your first week back to school after Christmas break?"

Elsie said, "It has been okay. I wish Christmas break had been longer, though."

Abby turned toward her and said, "Me too, but the good news is, my dad says that we might get snow tomorrow night. Maybe even enough to cancel school on Friday."

Elsie felt excited. She loved snow. "I hadn't heard that. It would be nice to have a snow day. I would love to have a long weekend."

"Me too," said Abby.

Gladys, the children's choir director, walked in, clapped her hands, and said, "All right, my friends, we have some fun new music to learn. Our choir will sing in church on the first Sunday in February. We are also going to start learning music for Bible School. I'll email your parents the link to the website."

Elsie loved Vacation Bible School. Her favorite part was always the music. Gladys gave her a solo for Bible School each year.

They worked on the song for February first. The song was called "God is Love" by Ginny Owens. Gladys played the song for the students and then said, "Does anybody know what is so special about Ginny Owens?"

No one was able to guess the answer, and eventually Gladys told them, "Ginny Owens is blind. Who else do we know that is blind?"

The kids all shouted, "Elsie!"

Abby leaned toward Elsie and said, "That's really cool that someone like you has recorded music."

Elsie wanted to groan. She hated when people compared her with other blind people. She also wondered why the coolest thing about Ginny Owens was that she was blind and recorded music. She said, "Yes, that's really cool. It's nice to hear about a blind person who is successful."

What Elsie *wanted* to say was, *Her music is very pretty, but I do not see how being blind and recording albums is any cooler than anyone else who records music. I think the most amazing thing about her is that she was determined to get her music noticed.*

When they had worked on "God is Love" for a while, Gladys said, "Let's talk about Bible School. This year we have a farm theme. We'll listen to a few of the songs today, and next week, we'll work on learning them."

As they listened, Elsie was not sure what she thought of the songs. They all seemed so different than the songs they usually had. But as she thought about the difference in the songs, she realized that it was not the songs that were changing. *She* herself was changing.

She felt sad when she realized this would be her last year to partici-pate in Bible School. Next year she would have to be a helper, and she was not sure what she could do to help. She could help with the music. Elsie decided to ask Gladys about it.

After they listened to a few of the songs, Gladys said, "My friends, it is time for you to go downstairs to midweek. I will see you next week."

As Elsie and her grandma left the sanctuary, Gladys stopped her and said, "I will email the website to your grandma."

"If I give you my email address, could you email *me* the link?" Elsie said.

"Oh," Gladys sounded surprised at that. "Sure. Let me go get a pen and paper."

Elsie wondered why Gladys sounded shocked. *Was it really that surprising that she could send emails*?

When Gladys returned, Elsie spelled out her email address. As much as she loved her grandma, she needed to start doing things on her own.

When Gladys was finished writing, she said, "I will email you *and* your grandma. I can also email you some of Ginny Owens's songs."

Elsie was annoyed. She had given Gladys her email address because she wanted to do more things on her own without help from her parents or Grandma Sally. Elsie wished that she could tell Gladys not to send the songs to Grandma Sally, but she thought that would be disrespectful. She finally said, "That would be nice. She has a pretty voice."

Gladys patted her back and said, "I will see you Sunday, my friend."

Chapter 14
Epiphany

There were three midweek classes. One was for kindergarteners and first-graders, one for second- and third-graders, and the last one was for fourth- and fifth-graders. Sixth-graders took confirmation classes on Wednesday night. The middle and high school students had their own choir. They had class while the kids had choir.

Elsie thought that it was silly to have confirmation classes on Wednesday night, because a lot of the kids could not come due to sports or other commitments. She could not count the number of times Grandma Sally had said, "Kids just don't have time for God today. Sports have become their God." But Elsie did not always agree with Grandma Sally. She thought that it was important to be available for God, but she did not think that time with God had to be in a church.

There were only four kids in Elsie's fourth- and fifth-grade midweek class. Abby and Eli were there, along with a shy boy named John. John did not attend choir because he did not like to sing in front of people.

Their midweek teacher, Karen, was Eli and Abby's mom. Karen made the twins miss soccer practice every Wednesday night. She always told them, "If your teachers and coaches don't understand that God comes first, then they aren't godly people. I don't want my children influenced by ungodly people."

When they got settled, Karen asked them, "Do you know what Epiphany is? And I don't want to hear from Abby or Eli, because I already know that they know."

Elsie said, "Epiphany is when the wise men brought gifts to baby Jesus."

Karen said, "Very good, Elsie!" in a squeaky, high-pitched voice, as if she were talking to a baby or a dog. Elsie *hated* when people talked to her in a baby voice. She wondered if Karen was surprised every time, she got an answer right. She was sure she would get answers right a lot, because Grandma Sally had a book of Bible stories that she read to her grandkids.

Karen's voice dropped back down to normal when she started talking to the rest the class. "The wise men followed a star to find Jesus. How do we find Jesus?"

John said, "But we don't have to find Jesus. We know that He's with God in Heaven."

Karen said, "Well, that is true, but what I mean is, we all have different things that help us feel closer to Jesus. Some of the things that help *me* feel closer to Jesus are working in my garden and sewing."

Abby said, "I feel close to Jesus when I am dancing."

Elsie said, "I love singing. I feel close to Jesus when I am singing."

"You have *such* a beautiful voice to glorify Jesus with," Karen squeaked.

Elsie had to work hard not heave a huge sigh. It was a wonder Karen did not have every dog in the neighborhood howling with how loud and high-pitched her voice was. Elsie had tried talking to Grandma Sally about the way Karen talked to her, but Grandma Sally did not think that Karen talked to her any differently than she did to the others.

"John? Eli?" Karen asked. "What makes you feel closer to Jesus?"

Eli said, "I feel close to God when I'm fishing."

John said, "I feel close to God when I'm playing baseball. I feel thankful that I can play baseball and that brings me closer to Jesus. Besides, my dad always prays with me before a big game."

Karen said, "John, playing baseball doesn't bring you closer to Jesus. You need to think of something else. Now, I brought large paper stars for everyone. Write down what makes you feel closer to Jesus on your star, and then you can decorate it."

Grandma Sally took a star for Elsie and said, "I'm guessing that you want to put singing on your star?"

"Yes. I want to put singing on my star and put musical notes on it."

Karen handed out paints and glitter to the students. Grandma Sally helped Elsie write *singing* in blue paint on the star, and then draw music notes in green, yellow, and pink paint. When they were finished painting, Grandma shook glitter over the whole thing.

While they worked, Elsie thought about how uncomfortable Karen made her. Elsie had slowly come to realize that she was the only student that Karen was nice to except for her own kids. It was as if Karen thought that Abby and Eli were perfect, and everyone else were not.

Elsie remembered that Karen had been mad at Gladys because she thought Abby and Eli should play the lead shepherd and angel, but Gladys had given those roles to Amanda and John. Elsie wondered why Karen had not been mad when Elsie got a bigger solo than Abby. She almost wished that Karen would be mean to her, because she knew that Karen was only nice to her because she was blind.

Elsie had to bite her lip to keep from laughing when she wondered if Karen had the "Karen haircut." Elsie's mom said that the "Karen haircut" was like a pixie cut. It was shorter in the back and longer in the front, and the bangs were usually swept to one side almost covering the eye.

Elsie's mom had told her about the Karen hairstyle because Mom had been laughing with Dad at dinner when she told him that Marsha had gotten the "Karen cut." Dad had laughed when Mom told him that Pam said it was fitting, because Marsha was always asking to talk to a manager when something did not go her way.

When everyone finished decorating their stars, Karen said, "Let's see what you came up with." She looked at Elsie's and said, "This is beautiful! Why don't you tell us about it."

"I put 'singing'," Elsie said, "because I love singing, and singing brings me closer to God."

When it was John's turn, Karen sighed. "I don't understand how your dog brings you closer to Jesus."

John took a breath and said, "My dog makes me happy when I'm sad. Doesn't Jesus make us happy when we are sad? Maybe my dog is helping Jesus with His work."

Karen *hmphed* and said, "Eli, let's see what you came up with."

Eli said, "I put fishing because when I am fishing, I think about how Jesus told the disciples to be fishers of men."

Karen smiled. "That is lovely. Abby, what about you?"

Abby said, "I put dancing, because dancing can bring glory to God just like singing."

Karen said, "Very good. Now, it's time for star cookies and juice."

As they ate their cookies and drank their juice, Elsie thought about John. She felt sorry for him. She completely agreed that dogs brought you closer to God. Elsie thought that it was not just dogs that did God's work. All pets helped do God's work of bringing joy to people.

She did not have a pet, but her Grandma Cara had a dog named Beethoven. She loved snuggling with Beethoven. He made her happy when she was sad. Her Aunt Tammy had a cat named Midge. She did not go over to her aunt's house much, but she loved Midge. She was fluffy and fun to snuggle.

When they were finished with their cookies and juice, it was time to get ready to leave. "Before you leave, let's all say a quick prayer," Karen said. "Everyone, fold your hands, bow your heads, and close your eyes."

When the prayer was over, Grandma Sally patted Elsie's arm and said, "I'm going to help Karen clean up." Elsie heard her grandma rip a paper towel off the roll and start wiping the table. "Abby, Eli, take the art supplies and leftover juice and cookies out to the car. John, is your mom here?"

"She said she'd wait for me upstairs."

Before John could leave, Elsie told him, "I agree with you. All pets help do God's work."

John sniffed and said, "Thanks, Elsie."

Grandma Sally came to her and said, "Are you ready to go, girl?"

Elsie sighed. "I guess I'm ready to go finish my reading."

Grandma Sally patted Elsie's arm. "Just get it done." When they got out to the car, Grandma asked, "What do you want to do with your star?"

Elsie shrugged. "I don't really care. You can keep it at your house."

"Mom would probably throw it away. Besides, the glitter will make a mess."

Grandma Sally opened the passenger door for Elsie. "Why did you put glitter on it?"

Elsie climbed in the car and shrugged before buckling her seat belt. "I like glitter. I just don't know what to do with my star now."

Grandma Sally shut the car door and got in on the driver's side. When she pulled into Elsie's driveway, she opened the car door and said, "Maybe I should start emailing you and saying, 'Do well in school.' I wish you would put as much effort into your schoolwork as you put into your music."

Elsie yawned and said, "I like music more than I like schoolwork."

Grandma Sally walked Elsie to the front door and gave her a hug. "Do you think Ginny Owens made excuses when she was in school?"

Elsie made the same sigh-growl noise her mom made when she was frustrated. "How should I know what she did or didn't do in school?"

Grandma Sally playfully smacked Elsie's arm and said, "She had a lot of determination to get things done. She had to if she wanted to get her songs noticed. Don't you think that she was just as determined in her schoolwork?"

Elsie sighed and said, "I guess so."

"I know you can do better."

Elsie hugged Grandma Sally tight, and said, "I'll try."

"That's all I ask for."

Chapter 15

New Possibilities

The next day after English, Shaylyn asked, "You won't be on the bus today, right?"

"No," Elsie said. "I have to work with Julie again."

"What are you and Julie working on today?"

"She's teaching me how to use a braille note-taker."

"What's that?" Shaylyn asked as Elsie picked up her book and unfolded her cane.

"It's kind of like a computer, except instead of having a computer keyboard, it has the same six keys that are on my braille writer."

"That sounds cool. It was cool seeing you use that thing to write today. It's kind of loud, but it's so cool seeing the dots pop up on the page."

"Thanks. I will see you tomorrow, ok?" Elsie did not want to be rude, but she knew that she had to hurry and get to the classroom and get her stuff packed up so she would not keep Julie waiting.

As she walked down the hall to Mrs. Perry's office, she heard the loud embosser. Mrs. Perry was probably brailling out some of her future worksheets. The embosser worked like a printer, except instead of printing things in ink, it brailed them.

When she walked into Mrs. Perry's room, she sat down in one of the chairs across from her desk. After she finished embossing, Mrs. Perry turned to Elsie and said, "I saw you stop and talk to Shaylyn on your way out of Mr. Dean's room. I'm glad you are making new friends."

"I like Shaylyn," Elsie agreed. "She is a nice girl."

"I'm glad you have someone to sit with on the bus."

"I am too. I didn't think I would want to sit with anyone at first, but I realized that it is fun to have someone to talk to." When Elsie heard footsteps in the hall, she guessed that it was Julie. She could tell that whoever it was had been outside because it sounded like the shoes were wet. She knew she had guessed correctly when the footsteps walked into the office, and she heard Julie's voice.

"How are we doing today, ladies?"

"We're doing well." Normally, Mrs. Perry left Elsie and Julie alone in her office, but she was staying for their lessons on the braille note-taker so she could help Elsie if she needed it next year.

After two hours of working on how to use the braille note-taker, it was finally time to go. "This thing is pretty cool," Julie said. "I think Elsie will enjoy being able to both read braille and listen to the voice at the same time."

"We already talked about that. Elsie can use the voice to read some books, but she must read her English books," Mrs. Perry said. She stood up and put on her coat while Julie put the braille note-taker back in her bag and Elsie put on her coat and grabbed her backpack.

"Well at least she can't pretend that she doesn't know it is upside-down." Julie put a hand on Elsie's shoulder. "Why did you do that?"

Elsie hung her head and said, "I don't know," in a voice so small it barely be heard.

They walked out to the car in silence, but once they were in the car, Julie turned to Elsie and said, "I don't believe that you don't know why you pretended you didn't know your book was upside-down."

Elsie sighed. "There are these girls in my class that I really want to be friends with: Amy and Krista. I have wanted to be friends with them *forever*. When Mrs. Conklin called on me to read after Amy, I was afraid of what Amy would think of me if I read slowly. I decided that it would be easier if I pretended, I couldn't find my place in the book."

Julie was quiet for a minute. "Do you have any friends at school besides Amy and Krista?"

Elsie leaned her head against the headrest. "There's a boy named Tanner that sits with me before school and at lunch, and a girl named Shaylyn who's in my reading class and on my bus. We started sitting together, but I don't know if either of them is my friends."

"Would you like to make some friends who are blind like you?" Julie asked.

Elsie felt scared. Was Julie going to suggest she go to the school for the blind? "Yes, I would like to make friends who are blind, but I don't want to go to the school for the blind."

Julie put a calming hand on Elsie's arm. "I'm not suggesting the school for the blind. I think it would be a good idea for you to go to summer camp."

"I'd like to go to camp. I've heard other kids talk about camp, but I thought there weren't any camps I could go to."

"There's one called Camp Silver Lake that I think would be good for you. I'll email you and your parents some information about it."

When Julie pulled up in front of Elsie's house, her dad was outside to meet them. "How did she do today?" he asked.

"She did fine. We talked about her reading upside-down the other day. She told me about Amy and Krista. I think it would be good for her to go to camp and make friends who are blind. She really hasn't had a chance to meet other kids who are blind."

Dad took Elsie's backpack and led her towards the house. "I think it would be good for her to go to camp, but her mom and I didn't know that there were camps she could go to."

"I will email you a link to Camp Silver Lake. I think Elsie would really enjoy it."

"Thank you. I know camp would be good for her."

"I will see you on Tuesday, Elsie," Julie said. "I want to get home before the snow comes. I don't like the look of those clouds."

*

When they went inside, Dad got out Elsie's braille writer and paper.

"We probably won't have school tomorrow," she said. "Can't I do my homework on Sunday?"

"Do we ever let you put your homework off until Sunday?"

Elsie sighed. "No."

"If we don't let you put your homework off on the weekend, what makes you think that you could put it off when we don't even know if there is going to be a snow day?"

Elsie slumped into a chair. "Wishful thinking."

Dad laughed. "Nice try, but it doesn't look like you have much, so just get it done and then you can have the rest of the night, and maybe even the rest of the weekend, to do what you want."

"Okay," she agreed.

He was right; she did not have much homework, and she was almost finished when her mom got home. Mom greeted Elsie by touching the back of her neck with her cold hands.

"Brr!" Elsie shivered. "Your hands are cold."

"You know what they say," Mom teased. "Cold hands, warm heart."

"Is it snowing yet?"

"Not yet. It's not supposed to start until around midnight."

"So, will we probably have school?" Elsie asked.

"That depends on how hard it snows. The last time I checked the weather, they said that we could get some sleet before the snow that could make the roads slick. Once it starts snowing, it will snow hard until noon tomorrow."

"I hope we don't have school."

"If you don't have school tomorrow, you'll have to make up for the snow day some other time," Mom reminded her.

"I still think a snow day would be fun."

When Elsie was getting ready for bed, she put on her pajamas with snowflakes on them. It was a tradition for their family to all get the same pajamas to wear on Christmas Eve. This year Elsie had been with her mom when she was looking at the pajamas, and Elsie got to help pick them out. She chose the pajamas with snowflakes on them because the snowflakes were raised and felt like they were made of glitter. Elsie loved anything with glitter because of the texture. Once she was in her pajamas, she grabbed the bunny that Julie had given her. Dad came in to kiss her goodnight and laughed.

"Do you think that if you wear snowflakes, the snow will come?"

"I'm doing everything I can to encourage it."

Elsie's mom walked in and said, "You're encouraging something. Do you hear that?"

Everyone got quiet, and Elsie could hear a small tap-tap against the window.

"Is that sleet?"

"Yep, and it's sticking to the car."

Elsie sat down on the bed with a bounce. "Cool!"

"It's not cool for me and your mom," Dad said. "We don't like scraping ice off our cars."

"I hate driving in the snow," Mom added. "It makes me nervous."

"It sucks that snow makes it hard to drive, but I want a snow day."

Elsie's dad laughed. She laid down, and he pulled the covers up over her and kissed the top of her head.

"Good night, sissy," he said.

"Good night, Dad. I love you."

"I love you, too," he said, and Elsie heard him walk out of the room.

Mom walked over to the bed, smoothed the hair back from Elsie's face, and gave her a kiss. "I love you. I'll see you in the morning."

"I love you, too."

And Elsie fell asleep thinking of snow.

When she woke up, she could hear the wind howling and smell her dad's aftershave. Dad had to be at work at five o'clock in the morning, so he was up long before anyone else was. Elsie knew she had a few more hours to sleep, so she rolled over and tried to go back to sleep. She heard her dad get his lunch out of the fridge and go outside. As she drifted off, she wondered if they had gotten any snow, and if they would have school.

Chapter 16
Frosty The Snowman

When Elsie woke up again, Mom was shaking her shoulder. "Elsie! There's a lot of white fluffy stuff outside."

Elsie yawned and stretched. "Do we have school?

"No, you're going to Linda's house along with your brother. She texted me and said that you guys should bring your snow gear, because you're going to play in the snow."

Elsie sat up and swung her legs out of bed. "Yes!"

Mom laughed. "There are clothes on the end of your bed. Get dressed and brush your teeth. You'll eat breakfast at Linda's house."

Elsie stepped out into the garage and slipped her feet into her boots. Even though they were fur-lined, her boots were still cold from being in the garage. She wondered why her mom could not put all the shoes in the house somewhere; there was nothing worse than cold shoes.

When Elsie climbed into the car, she was thankful that Mom had already come out and turned on her seat warmer. She heard her mom buckle Blake into his booster seat and shut the door. After Mom got in the car Blake said, "Mommy, we need music."

"No music today. Mommy needs to concentrate. The roads are slick, and it is hard to see."

At Linda's house, Elsie was disappointed to find that someone had shoveled the path to the doorway. She loved the "crunchy" sound the snow made when you stepped on it.

Linda opened the door, and Elsie could immediately smell maple syrup and bacon.

"Hi guys, come on in. We are having waffles and bacon for breakfast. I used my waffle-maker shaped like a snowman since we're going to make real snowmen later today."

Blake said, "We always get the waffles out of a box. Why don't you ever make snowman waffles, Mommy?"

"Mommy doesn't have time to make waffles," Mom said. "Now, you guys have fun playing in the snow. Daddy will pick you up when he gets off work."

Linda ushered Elsie and Blake to the table loaded with food as Mom drove back down the snowy road. Elsie could tell that Landon and Macey, another brother and sister that Linda babysat, were already there; she heard them talking and eating when she went into the dining room. Elsie knew that both of their parents were surgeons because Macey always wanted to play surgery. Macey had told her that "Mommy and Daddy save lives, and I want to save lives like them when I get big." Elsie guessed that their parents had surgeries that they could not reschedule today.

Feeling for her plate, Elsie took a bite of bacon and said, "This bacon is really good. It's crispy and crunchy, just the way I like it."

"Thank you," said Linda. "Take a bite of waffle and tell me what you think. I just got this waffle-maker at an after-Christmas sale."

Elsie stabbed a bite of waffle and popped it into her mouth. "This is the best waffle I've ever had."

Linda laughed. "I'm glad you like it."

"Where are Bridget and Michael?" Elsie asked. Bridget and Michael were Linda's own children, and it was unusual to not hear them talking with the other kids at Linda's house.

"Michael went to help his grandpa shovel snow, and Bridget is up in her room. You probably won't see much of her today."

Elsie hated that Bridget did not want to play with her anymore. Bridget was only a year older than Elsie, but since she started going to middle school, she acted like Elsie was just another annoying kid that her mom babysat. This hurt Elsie because she and Bridget had always been close. Elsie was one of the first kids Linda babysat, and that meant Elsie spent a lot of time with Bridget, until this year. But at the beginning of the school year, Bridget changed; she was always online, either posting on social media or playing a game with her friends.

Elsie was not sure what game Bridget was playing, but most popular online games were not accessible for people with visual impairments, and it made her feel left out. She wondered if there was an online game that she and Bridget could both play? But even if they *could* play a game together, Elsie was not sure that Bridget would play with her. She still had not accepted her friend request on Facebook, and Elsie could not help but think that it was because Bridget did not want to be friends with someone her mom babysat anymore.

After Elsie ate, she went into the living room and put her headphones on. She checked her email account and found emails from Gladys and Julie. She opened Gladys's email first. Gladys had sent her the Bible School songs and the songs by Ginny Owens. She decided she would listen to them later. But before she could open Julie's email, Linda interrupted her.

"Everybody put on your snow pants, hats, coats and gloves," Linda ordered. "It's time to go outside."

Out in the frigid air, Elsie was surprised to feel heavy snowflakes falling on her. "Was it snowing this hard when Blake and I got here?"

"No, it wasn't snowing when you guys got here," Linda answered. "It has been snowing off and on all morning."

Macey asked, "Miss Linda, are we going to build a snowman?"

"Yes, Macey. I brought a hat and some buttons for the eyes, and a carrot for the nose. You guys build the snowman, and Elsie will put on the face."

Elsie listened to the kids fighting about how to make the snowman; it was hard not to laugh at the things they said to each other.

"You have to make the balls bigger," Blake insisted. "Frosty can't be a baby snowman!"

"Who says Frosty can't be a baby snowman?" Macey argued.

"Frosty is a big snowman!" Landon insisted

Linda sighed and went to break up the fight. "Landon and Macey. You need to stop fighting and let the other kids help. Blake and Elsie want to help build the snowman as well. There's enough snow to make more than one snowman if you want."

Macey said, "We only have one hat, and the hat has the magic that makes the snowman come to life."

Elsie wondered what Linda would say to that.

"Let's make the big snowman, and then we can make some little ones if you guys want to," Linda told Macey. "You might be cold by the time we make the snowman and take pictures for your parents."

Elsie listened as Linda continued to show the kids how to build their snowman. When they were finished, Linda led Elsie over to the snowman and placed something hard and pointy in her hand. "Here is the carrot for Frosty's nose," she said.

Elsie took the carrot, and then reached out and touched the snowman. "Is his head going to be too small for the hat?"

Landon shouted, "I told you Frosty needed a bigger head!"

"His head is fine," Linda said patiently. "I brought a baby doll hat."

Macey said, "You have to bring a hat with magic in it so Frosty can talk."

Elsie stuck the carrot in the place she thought the nose would be. She could not understand why the kids were laughing.

Macey exclaimed, "You put Frosty's nose on his forehead!" But then she gently took Elsie's hand and said, "I'll help you fix it, Elsie."

Once the nose was in the right place, Linda handed Elsie one of the buttons.

"She's, my sister!" Blake shouted. "I want to help her with the eyes!"

Landon argued, "You get to help her all the time at home! I want to help her now!"

"We are going to let Elsie try to figure it out herself," Linda told them all.

Elsie gently felt where the nose was and placed the eye on one side of the nose. She knew she had gotten it right when the kids clapped, and Linda handed her the other button. She gently felt where the first eye and nose were, and then pressed the button into the snow on the other side of Frosty's face.

Macey jumped up and down. "Time for the hat! The hat has the magic that will make Frosty talk!"

Elsie's stomach sank as Linda handed her the hat. She carefully placed it on the top of Frosty's head, trying hard not to knock his eyes and nose off in the process.

"Let's get a picture of all of you with Frosty," Linda said when Elsie finished. She arranged everyone in a circle around Frosty and told them to smile for the picture.

"Miss Linda, why isn't Frosty talking?" Macey asked.

"Macey, snowmen don't really talk," Linda said patiently.

"But Frosty's hat is supposed to be magic," Macey whined.

Elsie could tell that Macey was about to cry, and almost cried with her. "When I was little, my papaw told me that you could hear Frosty talk with your heart, and that was the true magic of Frosty," she told the younger girl.

"So, there isn't any magic in the hat?" Macey asked as she tried to keep from crying. "What if you got a different hat?"

Landon said, "Snowmen can't talk, stupid. That's just a thing from a dumb movie."

Linda sounded sad when she said, "Landon, you need to be nice. Elsie is right. Frosty's magic is not in the hat. Frosty gets his magic when you believe in him."

There was silence, and Elsie could hear the snow falling. She loved the sound of snow falling, but she only heard it when everyone was quiet— which did not happen very often.

Finally, Macey asked, "So Frosty talks to me and I hear it with my heart?"

"Yes," Linda told her. "Frosty talks to you in your heart."

Chapter 17

Change

The rest of the day at Linda's house dragged by. Elsie was glad she had her phone, but she wished she could have stayed at home. It was hard to listen to music or watch a movie because the other kids were so loud. Also, watching a movie on her phone would quickly drain the battery. If she were at home, she could plug her phone in and keep watching her movie. She decided to talk to her parents about staying home by herself over summer break.

Elsie had not ever thought about staying home by herself before. It felt strange to think that she might be able to do something besides go to Linda's house during the summer. What would it be like to stay home by herself. She did not think she would be scared; she knew that her parents would lock all the doors before they left, and she would not open them for anyone. Her parents both had garage-door openers, so they would not need her to let them in. And it would be fun to play her music as loud as she wanted, with no one to tell her to turn it down.

What her parents would think of her staying home alone? Would they say she was too young? And if they did, would she have to suffer more days of boredom at Linda's house? Elsie loved Linda, but she did not want to spend another summer at her house, especially now that Bridget did not want to play with her anymore. Elsie could already imagine how bored she would be without someone close to her age to play with.

Thinking about having a friend her own age to play with made Elsie wonder what other kids in her grade were doing over the summer. *Were some of them staying home by themselves?* She had not heard anyone talk about summer plans yet. In the past, kids talked about going to camp and summer school. Some went on fun vacations with their families.

A few other kids talked about having Vacation Bible School at their churches. In the past, Vacation Bible School had been the best part of Elsie's summer, but after hearing the new songs on Wednesday, Elsie was not as excited as she used to be. It made her sad to realize that she was growing up, and the things that had always been fun, were not as fun anymore.

Elsie was happy when she heard her dad's voice at the end of the day.

"It's stopped snowing, but the temperature is dropping," he said as the door closed behind him.

"I'm sure you'll be happy to get home early," Linda said. "Elsie, Blake, your dad is here."

Elsie had just finished her snack, and she stood up from the table, grabbed her phone and headphones, and walked over to her dad.

"But I want to play race car with Landon!" Blake argued.

"You can play cars on Monday," Dad said. "Right now, I want to get home."

When they got outside, Dad put Elsie's hand on her car door and then went to buckle Blake into his booster seat. As Elsie waited for him to buckle in her brother, the wind blew in through Dad's open door and she shivered in the cold.

When Dad got in the car, Elsie said, "I have something I want to talk to you and Mom about over dinner."

"Okay. What is it?"

"I want to wait and talk to both of you together," she said.

"Alright, we'll wait and talk about it over dinner."

At home, they ate chicken strips and French fries because Mom and Dad were both tired and wanted something quick and easy.

"What did you want to discuss with us, Elsie?" Dad asked as he squirted ketchup onto his plate.

Elsie took a deep breath. "I'm tired of going to Linda's house."

"What's wrong with Linda's house?" he asked. "It sounded like you guys had a lot of fun today. When I came to pick you up, Linda said that you both had a good time making a snowman."

Mom took a drink and set down her glass. "That picture Linda sent looked like you guys were having lots of fun."

"I had fun at Linda's house today, Mommy," Blake said. "Elsie is just boring. All she did was play on her phone. She didn't play with us."

"I didn't *want* to play with you guys," Elsie said. "Your games are boring."

"They are not!"

"You two stop fighting!" Dad ordered.

Elsie could tell he was annoyed and chose her words carefully. "It isn't really that there is anything wrong with Linda's house; it's just that Bridget is the only one close to my age. She does not want to play with me anymore because she thinks she is better than me now that she goes to middle school. It was better today because I had my phone, but it's still boring at Linda's house."

There was silence around the table while everyone ate their food and thought about what Elsie had said. Finally, Mom said, "Well, your dad and I weren't going to say anything to you yet, but I'm going to quit my job in May and stay home next year. Your dad is getting a raise."

"Mommy, what is a raise?" Blake asked as he took a drink.

"Daddy is going to get more money, and I am going to clean house for a few people to make extra money."

Elsie was happy for her dad. "Your boss finally listened to your ideas?"

"No. My boss is leaving, so I'm taking his job."

"So that means that neither one of us will go to Linda's house anymore?" Elsie was not sure how she felt about this. She had been looking forward to staying home by herself.

"I was going to have you both go to Linda's house while I clean houses," Mom said, "but Elsie, I guess you could stay home. It would only be two days a week in the morning."

Elsie was excited at the thought. She would get to spend a little time on her own.

"Can I stay home with Elsie?" Blake asked.

"No, you're too young to stay home by yourself."

Her brother sniffed, and Elsie knew that the waterworks were about to start. "It's not fair that Elsie can stay home on her own and I can't!" he whined.

Elsie's dad started picking up the empty plates and cups. "Elsie is older than you."

Blake started to cry. "It's not fair!"

Elsie's mom sighed. "I think it is time for you to take a bath and get ready for bed."

"No!"

Mom sighed again. "Come on. I can tell you are tired." She must have picked Blake up and carried him out of the room because his cries got farther and farther away.

As Elsie helped her dad wash dishes, she thought about what her parents had just told her. She was happy that her dad was getting his boss's job; she knew that her dad's boss was the only reason he did not like his job.

Elsie was relieved she would not have to be bored at Linda's house this summer. She was also a little confused, because she was sad that she would be saying goodbye to Linda. *Hadn't she wanted to not go to Linda's house?*

As she scrubbed a sticky spot of barbecue sauce off a plate, she thought more about Linda. Elsie realized that she could not remember a time when she did not go to Linda's house. Linda had been babysitting her since she was a literal baby and felt like a member of the family. *When she stopped going to Linda's house, would she ever see her again?* Elsie did not want to think too much about it because she knew if she did, she would burst into tears.

As she washed the last cup, she realized that she still might not get to stay home by herself. She handed the cup to her dad and asked, "What if Julie wants to meet with me during the times Mom's cleaning houses?"

"Your mom will drop you off before she cleans."

"But then I won't get to stay home by myself."

Elsie heard her dad sit down in his recliner and put his feet up. "You have to work with Julie," he said.

"I know, but I was really looking forward to seeing what it's like to be by myself."

Dad did not say anything, and Elsie heard him scratch his head. Finally, he said, "Your brother's going to play soccer this spring, and I know that will not be any fun for you. As long as your mom's okay with it, you can stay home during the games."

"Thank you! I would be so bored if I had to sit through that."

"Do not get too excited. It is not a done deal yet. Your mom may think you need to go to the games and support your brother."

"I know, but…"

"Go get ready for your bath," Dad interrupted. "I want to talk it over with your mom."

Elsie grabbed her phone and turned on her Christmas playlist. It was not Christmas time anymore, but Elsie felt like she had to listen to Christmas music when it snowed outside.

"Don't play your music loud," Dad warned, "your mom just got your brother to sleep."

Elsie turned off her music and put her phone in her room. She decided that the first thing she would do when she got to be home alone was turn her music up as loud as she wanted. For now, she had a lot to think about, and a hot bath always helped her think.

Chapter 18
Cooking with Grandma Sally

Elsie spent every Saturday night with Grandma Sally. It started when she was a baby. For the first three years of Elsie's life, her mom and dad had both worked on Saturday nights, so Elsie stayed the night with Grandma Sally and went to church with her the next day. When her parents stopped working on Saturday night, Elsie insisted that she was supposed to spend Saturday night with Grandma Sally, so the tradition continued.

Sometimes, her cousins stayed the night with Grandma Sally as well, but she liked it best when it was just Grandma Sally, Grandpa George, and herself. When she walked in this Saturday, Grandma Sally and Grandpa George were in the living room. She put her clothes on the bed in the guest bedroom, and then walked into the living room.

"Did you put the Christmas program on Facebook?" she asked.

"Yes, your dad helped me post it on Facebook when you all were over here for dinner last week."

"Can we watch it? I want to see how I did on my solo."

Grandpa George turned off his TV and went to play on the computer instead, while Grandma Sally grabbed her phone and pulled up the Christmas program. Before she pressed "play" she said, "I wish you would put as much effort into your schoolwork as you do your music."

Elsie huffed and rolled her eyes. "You said that on Wednesday."

Grandma Sally patted her arm. "I'm saying it again."

As they listened to the online video, Elsie loved pretending that she was one of the crowds watching the program instead of participating in it.

"Lizzy did such a good job with her lines," she said as she leaned against the arm of the couch and put her feet in Grandma Sally's lap.

Grandma Sally patted her foot. "Yes, she did a good job. Aunt Meg worked on it with her."

"Gavin did a good job as well, but Blake didn't seem like he liked it much."

"Blake may be a kid who doesn't like to sing, and that's okay. He has other talents, even if we don't know about them yet."

They listened to the rest of the program in silence. Elsie's solo was at the end. Gladys had taught her the first verse of "Silent Night" in the original German. After they listened to Elsie's solo, she said, "I think I did pretty well. I love the songs Gladys picks. I like the "God Is Love" song that we are learning at choir. You know, I hope that someday I can be a choir director like Gladys."

"In order to be like Gladys, you will have to work very hard," Grandma Sally said. "You'll have to do well in school and go to college."

Elsie considered that for a moment. She had never really thought about going to college because it seemed so far away.

Grandma Sally got up off the couch and said, "You should ask Gladys about college sometime. She will tell you what she had to study, and how hard she had to work. College is still a long way off for you, but it never hurts to have an idea of what you want to study. But right now, it's time to study making dinner."

"What are we having?" Elsie asked.

"We are having Ritz chicken and tomato rice."

Elsie licked her lips. "Can I help?"

"You can help me with the chicken, but there isn't much you can do to help with the rice."

Elsie heard the squeak of cabinet doors opening, and the "clackety" sound of Grandma Sally setting two bowls on the counter. "What are we putting in the bowls?" she asked.

"We are going to put butter in one and cracker crumbs in the other."

Elsie heard the fridge door open; she guessed that Grandma Sally was getting the butter. She heard Grandma scoop some butter out of the container and into the bowl.

"While this is in the microwave, you can pound these crackers into crumbs," Grandma Sally told her. She handed Elsie a sleeve of Ritz crackers and something that felt like a hammer.

"Why do I need to use a hammer to crush crackers?" Elsie giggled.

"It's not a hammer; it's a meat tenderizer. The crackers need to be crushed well, and this will help you make sure the crumbs are as small as they can be."

Elsie started to pound the crackers and discovered that she enjoyed the task a lot. It was satisfying to hit something as hard as she could.

"Be careful," warned Grandma Sally. "You're going to leave a mark on my table."

"Why do we have demolition going on in here?" Grandpa George asked as he walked into the kitchen.

Elsie laughed. "Grandpa George, I'm crushing up the crackers for our Ritz chicken."

"Yuck! I don't want any of that nasty stuff."

"George, go back in the other room," Grandma Sally ordered. "We have a few burgers in the fridge. I will cook one for you. Do you want any rice?"

"Yeah, I'll have a little rice."

Elsie felt hurt. "Why doesn't Grandpa George want any chicken?"

"Grandpa grew up on a farm and they raised chickens, so they ate a lot of chicken, and he does not like to eat it anymore. I knew that he might not want any chicken, so I made sure I made an extra burger in the fridge. You are the only one who will eat Ritz chicken with me, so I only make it when you are here."

Elsie smiled. "I don't think Mom and Dad like tomato rice, so I only get that when I am here."

"It works out for both of us then," Grandma Sally smiled.

When Elsie was finished crushing the cracker crumbs, Grandma Sally got the chicken strips out of the fridge.

"I had a few chicken breasts in the freezer," she told Elsie, "So I thawed them out and cut them in to strips. I could have bought some chicken strips, but this works just as well."

Grandma arranged the bowls and pan on the counter in front of Elsie and said, "The chicken is on the left. Next to the chicken you have the butter, next to that you have the cracker crumbs. Roll the chicken strips in the butter and then in the cracker crumbs. The butter will help the crumbs stick. Once they are covered, you can put them in the pan. The pan is behind the bowls."

Elsie picked up one of the chicken strips "They feel slimy!"

"That's because they're not cooked."

While Elsie prepared the chicken, Grandma preheated the oven. Elsie liked helping her grandma cook. She liked that her grandma showed her how to do things correctly. When she finished rolling the chicken in butter and cracker crumbs, she washed her hands and sat down at the kitchen table to wait until the oven was ready.

When the oven beeped, Elsie asked, "Can I put the chicken in the oven?"

"Sure, let me get you the oven mitts." Grandma Sally handed Elsie the oven mitts, and she slid them on. "Can you feel where the oven door is?"

Elsie felt down to where she knew the door was. "Yes."

"Open the door and pull out the rack."

Elsie opened the door and reached inside for the rack. She was glad she had the oven mitts on because the oven felt hot. She pulled out the rack like grandma said, and then stood up.

"The chicken is in front of you on the counter," Grandma Sally directed.

Elsie found the pan, but because the oven mitts were so thick, she had trouble picking it up. Finally, she managed it, and slid the pan into the oven.

"Push the rack in and close the door."

Grandpa walked back into the kitchen as Elsie pushed the rack in. "Do you think that she should be doing that?"

"She's not hurting anything, and I'm standing right here watching her."

"If she gets burned, her mama and daddy won't be happy."

Grandma Sally took a deep breath. "George, she put the pan in the oven and didn't get hurt. She is fine. Go in the living room and leave us alone!"

He left the room again, and Elsie sighed in relief. "I love Grandpa George, but he worries too much. Are you going to start the rice now?"

"I'm going to wait a minute before starting the rice because it doesn't take as long as the chicken to cook."

Elsie sat down in the dining room to wait, and when she heard Grandma get a pot out of the cabinet, she walked back into the kitchen. "I know there isn't really anything I can do to help, I just want to learn how you make it," she said.

Grandma handed Elsie a can and a can opener. "You can open this can of chicken broth."

Elsie put the can opener on the lip of the can and turned it on. She loved feeling it go round and round. "Why are we using chicken broth?" she asked.

"Chicken broth gives the rice more flavor. We're going to pour the broth in the pot and wait for it to come to a boil."

A few minutes later, Elsie heard the broth start to boil. "Do we pour in a whole box of rice?"

Grandma Sally laughed. "No, if we used a whole box of rice, we would have enough to feed an army! You have felt uncooked rice, it is smaller than cooked rice. When rice cooks, it expands. Two cups may not look like much right now, but once it's cooked, it will be enough for the three of us." Elsie heard Grandma pour the rice into the pot as she kept speaking. "Now we cover it with a lid and wait for five minutes. You can help me open these cans of tomato sauce while we wait."

"How much tomato sauce are we putting in there?"

"Just two. They're small cans."

After enough time had passed, Grandma took the lid off the pot of rice, and she dumped in the two cans of tomato sauce that Elsie had opened. "Now I am going to add some pepper to give it a little extra flavor," she said, and Elsie heard her dump a little bit of pepper into the rice and stir it.

When the oven timer beeped, Elsie asked "Can I get the chicken out of the oven?"

"Sure, let me get you the oven mitts."

Elsie put the oven mitts on and opened the oven door. She carefully reached for the rack and pulled it out. She was nervous because the oven was much hotter than it was when she put the chicken in, and this time the pan was hot too. She carefully pulled the pan out of the oven and set it on the counter, and then closed the oven door.

"You did a good job," Grandma Sally said. "We'll let the chicken cool a little while I heat up Grandpa's burger."

When Grandma and Elsie sat down to eat, Elsie tasted the chicken. "I did pretty good. I got just the right amount of cracker crumbs on it."

Grandma patted her hand and said, "Yes, you did. See what happens if you try?"

Elsie sighed and said, "Yes. I know what you're trying to say." Grandma laughed, and they ate their dinner.

Chapter 19
Collision Course

When they got home from church the next day, Elsie and Grandma both changed out of their dress clothes. It was time for Grandma Sally to start preparing Sunday lunch. Much like Elsie staying the night with Grandma Sally was tradition, Sunday lunch was a tradition that went back to when Elsie's mom, Aunt Meg, and Uncle Mark were kids. Mom often said, "It wouldn't feel like Sunday if we didn't have Sunday lunch."

"Can we bring the trikes upstairs and ride?" Elsie asked.

Grandma Sally thought for a minute. "I guess so, but you will need to be careful," she said. Then she went downstairs and brought up all the trikes.

Elsie was getting too big to ride a trike, but she liked having three wheels. She had ridden a bicycle once, and it was so wobbly that it scared her. She decided then that she would continue to ride her trike until she was too big for it. And Grandma Sally was nice enough to let her grandkids ride in the house when it was too cold to go outside.

When Mom, Dad, and Blake got there, Elsie rode into the living room to greet them. "Hi Mom, hi Dad."

Blake shouted, "I want to ride *my* trike!"

"Grandma brought it upstairs for you," Elsie said. Blake jumped on his trike, and he and Elsie rode down the hall.

When Elsie heard Aunt Meg and Uncle Mark walk in, she rode back into the living room. "Aunt Meg, will you braid my hair?"

"Sure," Aunt Meg said, "Come sit on the floor by me."

When Gavin and Lizzy, Elsie's cousins, saw their trikes, they shouted, "Yay, we can ride our trikes in the house today!" They rode down the hall to find Blake.

After Aunt Meg braided Elsie's hair, Elsie got back on her trike and rode down the hall to see what the others were doing. They were all gathered in the doorway to the playroom trying to decide what to play.

Gavin said, "I think we should play police car. My daddy is a police officer and I want to be one too."

Blake argued, "I don't want to play police car cause you're *always* the policeman." Gavin was five, and Blake and Lizzy were only three. Gavin tried to act like he was the boss when Elsie or their cousin Camille, who was eight, were not around.

Elsie sighed. She knew if she did not break up this fight, they would not get to ride their trikes in the house anymore. "Let's just ride up and down the hall, guys. We don't really need a game when we are riding our trikes." But after they rode their trikes up and down the hall for a little while, Gavin asked, "Can we please play police car?"

Elsie sighed. "I guess so."

Blake and Lizzy rode down the hall toward the playroom and Gavin chased them, yelling, "This is the police! Pull over now!"

Elsie rode her trike into the bathroom. She knew Gavin would be busy chasing Blake and Lizzy for a little while. If she kept quiet, he would forget about her until he had pulled both Blake and Lizzy over and given them tickets.

She listened as Gavin caught his sister, Lizzy, first. "I pulled you over, so now you have to pull into the playroom," he ordered. "That's where the bad guys go."

Lizzy started to cry. "I don't want to be in trouble!"

"Shhhh. Lizzy, it is just a game. Do not cry, or Mom and Dad will think I am being mean to you. You can come out as soon as I catch all the bad guys."

Lizzy stopped crying and rode into the playroom.

Once Lizzy was in jail, Gavin rode after Blake, who had driven into Grandma and Grandpa's room. "Come out of that house, bad guy. I see you trying to steal!"

Blake rode out of Grandma and Grandpa's room, and Gavin caught him and made him ride his trike into the playroom. There was silence for a minute before Gavin yelled, "Elsie? Where are you?"

Elsie knew that she had to get out of the bathroom before Gavin could corner her. She pedaled her trike as fast as she could up the hallway. When she was in the living room, she ran over something.

"Ouch! That was my foot!"

"Sorry Uncle Mark," Elsie said. "I didn't know you were there."

"Well, I hope you wouldn't run over someone you knew was there. Maggie, your daughter is a bad driver."

Gavin rode up the hall and said, "Elsie, I caught you! So now you get a ticket, and you have to go to jail with the other bad guys."

Uncle Mark laughed. "Elsie needs her license taken away. She just ran over my foot." Gavin laughed, and his dad continued, "You wouldn't think it was so funny if she ran over *your* foot."

Elsie's mom said, "It will be time for lunch soon, so everyone is going to lose their licenses."

Elsie got off her trike and rubbed her knees. She had not realized before what a tight fit it was. Her knees stuck straight up when she rode because there was not enough leg room on the trike. She felt sad when she realized that soon she would not be able to ride her trike anymore.

Riding her trike in the house gave her a sense of freedom. She did not like riding outside because she did not know where she was going.

When she rode in the house, she knew where everything was, so she did not crash into any walls. She never had to worry about the basement door because Grandma Sally made sure it was closed. Elsie thought she understood now why everyone said that she should not be in a hurry to grow up.

Elsie listened as her mom pushed her trike to the playroom and told Blake and Lizzy that it was time for everyone to get off their trikes.

"Gavin said I wasn't in trouble!" Lizzy wailed.

"Elsie ruined it for everyone. All of you go wash your hands and get ready for lunch. We will eat as soon as your aunt and uncle get here."

They all went and washed their hands, and when Uncle Mike, Aunt Jill, and Camille got there, they had meatloaf, mashed potatoes, and green beans for lunch.

Chapter 20
Can Drive

A few weeks later, there was an assembly in the school gym. Elsie loved assemblies, especially when they got her out of history class. It was one day that she would not have to try to keep up with the rest of the class while they were reading.

When they got into the gym, Tanner touched Elsie's arm and asked, "Can I walk you to where our class is sitting?"

"Sure." Elsie took his arm and walked with him.

"Okay, here is where we're sitting. If you sit down, you will be facing the stage."

Elsie was surprised that he had learned to guide her so quickly. Amy and Krista still occasionally ran her into something when they were guiding her. "What do you think the assembly is about?" Elsie asked as she sat down.

"I don't know, but I'm okay with anything that gets us out of history class," he said.

Elsie laughed. "I was thinking the same thing. I hate reading out loud, and history is boring."

Before Tanner could reply, the principal said, "Boys and girls, you need to turn your voices off. Mrs. Miller from the food bank is here to talk to us."

Elsie heard the principal's shoes clack on the floor as she walked away from the microphone. Next, she heard someone else step up to the microphone and adjust it. "Good afternoon, boys and girls. My name is

Mrs. Miller and I work at the food bank. Do any of you know what a food bank is?"

Elsie thought she knew what a food bank was but did not want to raise her hand and risk getting called on to answer the question. She was afraid that her answer would be wrong, and then she would not only be embarrassed in front of her class, but the rest of the *school* as well.

Someone else must have raised their hand, because Elsie heard a small voice say, "A food bank is a place where people go to get food when they don't have enough money to get food at the store."

"Yes, that's right." Mrs. Miller sounded pleased. "We give people all different kinds of food. We have everything: meat, fruit, and vegetables. We even have some snacks. You all like snacks, don't you?"

Everyone agreed that they did like snacks, but Elsie thought it was a dumb question. *What person did not like snacks?*

"We always have a can drive around Thanksgiving at your school. Did any of you participate in the can drive this year?"

Everyone in the school had participated in the can drive, because Elsie heard voices from all over the gym scream "Yeeesss!" She had participated in the can drive as well. She had asked for cans from everyone in her family and had gone around the neighborhood asking for donations.

Mrs. Miller sounded happy when she said, "That's great! We always have a lot of food around Thanksgiving and Christmas because people are in a giving spirit and very generous around that time of the year. However, around the end of January and beginning of February, when all our holiday food is gone, we sometimes have a little trouble getting enough food. Your principal and I thought that it might be fun to have another can drive. The class that collects the most cans will get extra recess. You all would like that, wouldn't you?"

Again, Elsie thought the question was silly. *What kid did not like extra recess?*

Beside her, Elsie felt Tanner stand up, and then heard his footsteps moving quickly out of the gym. Mrs. Conklin's shoes squeaked on the floor as she walked after him. Elsie could always tell when Mrs. Conklin was close because she always wore high heels. Mrs. Perry had once told Elsie that Mrs. Conklin wore the highest heels she had ever seen.

While Tanner and Mrs. Conklin were out of the room, Mrs. Miller went on talking about what kinds of things they needed most, and how they would put them in a special box in their classrooms. Elsie only half paid attention. She was too busy wondering because Tanner left the room. *Was he OK?*

A few minutes later, as Mrs. Miller finished her speech, Tanner walked back into the room, followed closely by Mrs. Conklin. He sat back down by Elsie, and she thought she heard him sniff. She wanted to ask him if he was all right but did not want to get in trouble for talking.

When the assembly was finally over, Elsie walked out of the gym with Tanner. "Are you OK?" she asked. "I heard you walk out of the gym during the assembly."

Tanner sniffed and said, "I'm fine."

"You sound sad. Are you sure you are, OK?"

"I'm fine."

When they got out of the gym, Elsie unfolded her cane and walked to class by herself. When she got to the classroom, it was time for her to go to Mr. Dean's room for reading.

*

That day, when Dad picked up Elsie and Blake from Linda's house, she told him about the can drive. "Mrs. Miller from the food bank came to talk to us about how they run low on food around January and February."

Her dad buckled Blake into his car seat and shut the door. When he got in, he said, "Yes, I can see how they would have a hard time collecting food this time of year. Mrs. Miller is right when she said that people are in a giving spirit around Thanksgiving and Christmas. Because they are thinking about giving, they know that it is good to give to those who are less fortunate than themselves. Some do it for the right reason: wanting to be a help to others. Other people do it because it makes them feel good about themselves."

Her dad started the car, and Elsie thought about this for a second. "I wonder if Tanner doesn't like to give to others?"

Her dad pulled out of the driveway and asked, "What makes you think that Tanner doesn't like to give to other people?"

"When Mrs. Miller was talking about the can drive, she said that the class that collected the most would get extra recess. And he walked out of the gym!"

Her dad thought about this as he drove. "I don't think it's fair to assume that Tanner walked out because he didn't want to give to others. There could be several other reasons why he walked out. Maybe he had to go to the bathroom, or get a drink, and it just couldn't wait till the end of the assembly."

"If he just went to get a drink or go to the bathroom, why did Mrs. Conklin walk out after him?" Elsie argued.

"Did he tell her where he was going before, he left?"

"No, I don't think so. He was sitting right beside me, and I do not know where she was sitting. He walked out of the gym so fast; I don't see how he would have time to tell her where he was going."

Dad reached into the center console and grabbed the garage door opener. She heard him press the button to open the door, and then the loud sound of the garage door opening. "She might have just been follow-ing him to see what he was doing. It is not polite to walk out in the middle of an assembly. And it is especially bad manners to leave without telling a teacher where you are going." Her dad pulled into the garage and turned off the motor.

Elsie still was not convinced that Tanner only left because he needed a drink or to go to the bathroom. They had had time to do that before the assembly. "It was also weird that when he got back, he was sniffing like he had been crying. Why would going to the bathroom or getting a drink made you sniff like you have been crying?" Elsie asked as she opened the car door, grabbed her backpack, and got out.

Her dad sighed. "Does it really matter? He did leave the room and cry. His mom gets some of their food at the food bank. He might have been embarrassed because he knows Mrs. Miller. He might have been crying because he knew that his family cannot afford to give away any of their food to others because they need it all themselves. If the class with the most cans at the end gets a free recess, he is afraid that the class will blame him if they do not win. It might be that he is the only kid in your class that cannot bring cans or any sort of food to the can drive. Think about how that would make you feel."

Elsie did think about it. She could understand now why Tanner walked out, and why he did not want to talk about it when she had asked. "I would be embarrassed if I knew Mrs. Miller because I think I would be afraid that she would say something to me, and other kids would ask how I knew her."

She walked with her dad and brother into the house. Dad took Blake into the living room to watch a movie, and Elsie went into the kitchen to start her homework.

When her dad walked into the kitchen, Elsie was taking her books out of her backpack. "I could bring a few extra cans and give them to Tanner, so he has something to put in the basket."

Dad flipped through her notebook. "You need to leave it alone. I know you are trying to help Tanner, but you will help him more by not saying anything."

Elsie had a challenging time focusing on her homework. She was still thinking about Tanner. *What would she want if she were in his place?* Part of her agreed with her dad that it would be better not to say anything. It might make Tanner feel bad if she offered to share some of what she brought. On the other hand, she knew *she* would feel bad if she did not have anything to put in the box; she would worry that people thought that she was selfish. Elsie decided that it would be harder for her not to have anything to put in the box than it would be for someone to see her taking something from someone else to put in the box.

When they had the can drive in November, the donation box had been right inside the classroom door. There were mornings when it was hard to get into class because everyone had brought something, and they all stood in the doorway to put their items in the box. Elsie remembered how she had liked having the box right inside the door because it was easy to find, but also because everyone could see how much she brought. That also meant that everyone could tell who *did not* bring anything.

Elsie felt bad for thinking that Tanner did not like giving to other people when she remembered how sad he had sounded today. She did not agree with her dad that she should just leave it alone. She decided that tomorrow morning she would ask Tanner if he would like to share some of what she brought. If he accepted her offer to share, Elsie decided she would not tell her dad she was sharing with Tanner. She would just give him some of her own cans.

Chapter 21
Singing in Church

On the first Sunday in February, Elsie sang in church.

The children's choir had been working on the song since choir had started at the beginning of January. Gladys had decided to break the song up into solos for the older children because she thought the song was too much for the little ones to learn.

Eli, Abby, and Elsie were the only kids singing. John did not care that he did not have a solo because he hated singing solos. Gladys said she would plan a song just for the little kids.

When they got to church, Grandma Sally walked her up to the choir loft where Gladys and the other kids were waiting. She put Elsie in the seat next to Abby, patted her back, and said, "Sing pretty. I will see you after."

Elsie did not like sitting in the loft. It was right beside the organ, and the organ was loud. She decided to think about other things while she waited for her turn to sing. She knew she should pay attention, but the sermon was *so* boring. She would make up for her wandering thoughts now by paying extra attention in Sunday School later.

Elsie wondered if she would ever find the sermons interesting. Their Sunday School lessons followed what the pastor talked about, but next year when she was in confirmation class, she would learn more about the beliefs of the Lutheran church. Elsie wondered if anyone else found the pastor's sermons dry. *How would she learn what he was talking about if she were too bored to pay attention to his sermons, and she wasn't in a Sunday School class that talked about what he preached?* She decided to save that problem for another day.

Elsie thought about Tanner instead. She loved that he talked to her before school and at lunch. She also thought about how close Valentine's Day was. She wished that he would ask to be her boyfriend. That would make this Valentine's Day the best.

She was pulled out of her daydream when Abby tapped her shoulder and whispered, "It's time to sing." She quickly stood up, and Gladys handed her the microphone. Her solo was first.

Elsie heard the piano start to play, and she listened for her cue to start singing. She was not nervous while singing; she had been singing since she could talk. When people asked her why she liked to sing so much, she always said, "I can't really explain it. It's like my soul has wings."

When the song was finished, Gladys walked her to where Grandma Sally was sitting. Gladys showed her where the seat was and said, "You did a good job."

Grandma Sally handed her a peppermint and said, "Good job." Elsie did not know why, but she liked sucking on peppermints after she finished singing. As she sucked on the candy, she continued to daydream about Tanner.

Thankfully, there was not much more of the sermon left. When the service was over, Elsie and Grandma started walking toward the door. She felt a hand on her shoulder. "Honey, you have such a beautiful voice to glorify God with."

Elsie smiled. "Thank you." She could not remember who that lady was, but she knew it was one of Grandma Sally's friends.

Several other people stopped her on the way out of church and congratulated her on her singing. When they got to the front of the church, the pastor shook her hand and said, "It is always a treat to hear the choir sing. You did a good job today."

Elsie smiled. "Thank you. I love getting to sing for God."

He patted her shoulder and said, "I know God is pleased with your singing voice."

Elsie loved singing for God, but if she was honest, she liked singing for herself just as much. She loved being told what a beautiful voice she had. In Sunday School, they talked about not being prideful and remembering to thank God for what they had. Elsie tried to remember to thank God, but sometimes she got caught up in all the compliments.

Chapter 22
Hopeful Friendship

The next day at lunch, Elsie sat between Amy and Krista. Tanner was not at school today, so Mrs. Lester had seated her beside the two girls. She had not eaten lunch with them lately because she had been sitting with Tanner in the cafeteria. She had been spending recess with him too; if he did not swing with her on the playground, he would help her to a swing and come back for her at the end of recess.

Even on days when Tanner did not swing with her, Amy and Krista did not come over to the swings to talk to her. Elsie had begun to wonder if asking about a sleepover at Amy's house had made them not want to talk to her. She was starting to think that Amy and Krista would never be her friends in the way she wanted them to be.

At least, she had thought that until today. Now, Amy and Krista included her in their conversation.

"I'm excited for Valentine's Day; my Daddy always gets me something nice," Amy said.

Elsie dipped a fry in catsup and said, "I'm excited for Valentine's Day too. I'm hoping that Tanner asks me to be his girlfriend."

Amy squealed. "Ooh, I hope he does too. You guys are so cute together!"

Elsie smiled. Finally, she was getting to talk to Amy and Krista like she had always wanted to.

Amy zipped up her lunch box and then asked, "Do your parents get you anything for Valentine's?"

"Dad usually gets me candy, and sometimes he gets me and my brother little gifts." Elsie said after finishing the last of her fries. She did not want to tell Amy and Krista that the small gift her dad gave her was usually some kind of stuffed animal. She did not know if Amy and Krista still played with stuffed animals, and she did not want to be embarrassed if they did not.

"My parents take me and my sister out to eat," said Krista. "Are you finished, Elsie? You can walk with me to put your tray away." Elsie stood up to walk with Krista, and as they walked Krista continued, "We've seen how Tanner takes your tray for you every day. I do not think Mrs. Perry would like that, do you?"

Elsie did not know what to say. Yes, Mrs. Perry wanted her to do as much for herself as she could, but she had not thought her aide would mind Tanner doing a cordial thing for her. *Should she tell Tanner that he could not take her tray to the dirty tray bin anymore?* She should confess to Mrs. Perry and hope she would not be too mad. Elsie knew that it would be better if she told Mrs. Perry before Amy or Krista did.

"I'll tell Mrs. Perry about it myself," Elsie said.

She heard the other girl put her tray in the bin, and then Krista said, "Walk straight ahead and the tray bin will be in front of you."

Elsie found the bin and sat her tray down. She took Krista's arm, and they walked back to the table.

"Amy and I just want to make sure that you're doing what you are supposed to do. We would hate for Mrs. Perry to be mad at you," Krista said as she put Elsie's hand on her chair.

Elsie sat and said, "Thank you." As she waited to go out to recess, her thoughts were buzzing about Amy and Krista. She had thought that they did not want to be her friends, but now they were including her in their conversations and trying to make sure she did not get in trouble. *Friends tried to keep their friends out of trouble, right?*

When they lined up for recess, Amy held her arm out for Elsie. "Krista and I want to show you a new game," she said. "Will you play with us?"

Elsie's heart leaped; Amy and Krista were inviting her to play with them! "I would love to," she said. There was hope for her friendship with Amy and Krista after all.

Chapter 23
Shaylyn to the Rescue

When they got outside, the weather was warm. Elsie held on to Amy's arm as they walked; she did not know where they were going, but they seemed to be heading away from the playground. Elsie was surprised when the crunching wood chips under her feet turned to grass. "Where are we going?" she asked.

"Krista and I want to take you to our special spot," giggled Amy. "It is a magical spot. We have to run, or the portal will close." Before Elsie knew what was happening, Amy started to run. She tried to keep up, but Amy was too fast.

The next thing Elsie knew, she was on the ground. She had tripped over something. *But what?* Her knee hurt, and something sharp poked her hand. She stood up and brushed herself off; her jeans were torn at the knee, and her fingers touched something sticky and wet. She wiped her fingers on her jeans, and Amy touched her shoulder.

"Oh, I'm sorry. Are you okay?"

"Yes, I'm fine," Elsie said, "but can we walk instead of running?"

"Sure," Amy agreed. "You tripped over the portal to our magic land. We'll be at our spot soon."

Elsie took Amy's arm again, and they walked on. As they moved, Elsie realized that she could not hear other children's voices. This made her nervous. *Were they still on the playground?* It felt as though she had gone through a magical portal.

Finally, Amy stopped and said, "Here we are. You can sit here. Isn't it peaceful?"

As she sat, Elsie realized that it *was* peaceful. Birds chirped happily around her. She wished she could tell them to not get so happy, because it was going to get cold again tonight; winter would not be over for a few more months, even though today felt like a spring day. The sun warmed her face, and Elsie loved the way it felt on her skin, like something warm was wrapped around her.

"Yes, it is kind of peaceful," she agreed. But neither Amy nor Krista said anything. "Amy? Krista? Where are you?" Elsie was getting scared. She did not know where Amy and Krista were, and she could not hear anyone else. *How would she line up with the others when recess was over?*

Then, "Ouch!" Something scratched her arm. Elsie touched the scratch. "Amy?! Krista?!"

Something scratched her other arm. Elsie felt slightly dizzy, as if she were floating above her body. She heard a small "snap," like someone had stepped on a stick. *Were Amy and Krista close?* Then something hit her knee, the one that was already hurt. She did not feel any pain, but she thought she felt something run down her leg.

Something else bounced off her forehead and landed in her lap. She picked it up but could not tell what it was. It was familiar, and yet not familiar at the same time. She put it in her pocket so she could figure out what it was later, when she did not feel so floaty.

"Amy? Krista? I want to leave now," she called. Footsteps crunched on either side of her.

"Hi Elsie," Amy said in a sing-song voice, "sorry Krista and I left you, but you stepped on a nest of one of the monsters that live here, and we didn't want them to attack us too."

Elsie stood up. She wished she had something to lean on because she still felt floaty. How was she standing up and floating above her body at the same time? "I don't believe in monsters," she said.

Amy snorted. "Well, you should, because when you stood up, you stepped on another nest. So now they are really, *really* mad at you."

Krista added, "Sorry Elsie, but they are coming back, and we don't want to be attacked."

Elsie heard their footsteps running away and heard Amy's snort-laugh. She sat back down and put her head in her hands. *Would anyone ever find her?* She did not know where she was, and she could not hear anyone else around her.

*

Elsie heard more footsteps, coming toward her this time. She did not think it was Amy or Krista, and she knew it was not one of their made-up monsters. *Did they really think she would believe that?* She could tell when someone reached her and stood beside her, but she did not think she could speak. A hand on her shoulder startled her.

"Elsie? Are you ok?"

"Shaylyn?"

Suddenly, Elsie was in her body again; she was not floating anymore. But now her knee hurt, her arms stung, and her stomach churned. Why did it feel like butterflies were throwing a party in her tummy?

"Are you okay?" Shaylyn asked her.

Elsie lifted her head. "I'm. . ." she was not sure how to answer that question. If she said she was okay, then Shaylyn might leave, and she did not want Shaylyn to leave. But if she said that she was not fine, she would have to explain what had happened, and she did not want to explain it to anyone.

"Hannah and Zoe have never made dandelion chains, so I came out here to see if I could find any," Shaylyn said. "I was pulling up dandelions when I saw those girls from your class running away from you."

Elsie touched a scratch on her arm. "They said that they wanted to play with me," she said in a shaky voice.

"Oh!" Shaylyn exclaimed. "Both of your arms are scratched, and your knee is bleeding."

Elsie touched her knee again; that explained the warmth she felt running down her leg. "My knee really hurts," she admitted.

Shaylyn touched her shoulder. "I think you should go see the nurse; your knee looks pretty bad. Come on, I'll walk with you."

Elsie stood and brushed off her pants. Her hand hurt as well. "We should probably find Mrs. Lester first. She will want to know where we are going," Elsie said as she took Shaylyn's arm. Soon she could hear other children's voices and feel the wood chips under her feet. She was relieved to be back on the playground.

It took Shaylyn a minute to find Mrs. Lester. She was breaking up a fight on the playground, and when she turned to them, Elsie could hear the concern in Mrs. Lester's voice.

"Elsie, what happened?" she gasped. "I saw you walk off with Amy and Krista. Where are they?"

Elsie swallowed hard before she answered. "They left me, and I don't know where they went."

Mrs. Lester was silent for a minute before she asked, "How did you get hurt?"

Elsie did not know what to do. She knew now that Amy and Krista were not her friends, but she still did not want to tell on them. Once she told Mrs. Lester what Amy and Krista had done to her, she would have no chance of being friends with them. Even though it was clear now that Amy and Krista did not *want* to be her friends, it was still hard to give up the dream of being invited to Amy's house to play with Princess. Even when Amy said that her mom would feel uncomfortable with Elsie coming to their house, she had still wished for an invitation.

She was afraid, too, that if she got them in trouble, she would be seen as the class tattletale. No one would want to be friends with the class tattletale. Amy and Krista were popular, and all the girls in class wanted to be friends with them. If they told everyone that Elsie was a tattletale, she might never be able to make friends.

And if she could not make friends, who would she partner with for group projects? She knew that Tanner had a group of boys that he partnered with, and she had always partnered with Amy and Krista, partially because they sat close to her, but also because it seemed like a clever way to make friends with them. She could not partner with them anymore, but who *would* she partner with if Amy and Krista said she was a tattletale. The class tattletale always got chosen last, and Elsie hated being chosen last.

Mrs. Lester cleared her throat and pulled Elsie from her thoughts. "Elsie? Can you tell me what happened?"

Elsie knew she would have to tell the whole truth at some point, but for now she decided to start with a half-truth. "Amy was walking too fast, and I tripped and fell."

"Hmm. I will have to find Amy and have a talk with her," said Mrs. Lester.

"Can I walk with Elsie to the nurse's office?" Shaylyn asked.

Mrs. Lester gave her permission, and the two girls walked to the nurse's office together. While they walked, Elsie tried to make sense of what had happened. She did not understand why Amy and Krista had been so mean to her. *Had she done something to offend them?*

"I'm sorry I didn't find you sooner," Shaylyn said quietly.

"I'm glad you found me when you did. Why are you sorry?"

Shaylyn was silent for a minute. "If I had found you sooner you might not have gotten hurt. You are going to tell the nurse what happened, aren't you?"

Elsie sighed. "Yes, I'll tell her what happened."

"You'll tell her *all* of what happened?" Shaylyn prompted.

"What do you mean?" Elsie asked.

"When I saw Amy and Krista, they were running away and holding sticks. I am guessing that is how you got the scratches on your arms. Did you really trip?"

"Yes, I tripped over something, but I don't know what it was," Elsie said. "Amy said I tripped over the portal to their magic land, but I don't believe that."

When they reached the nurse's office, Shaylyn put Elsie's hand on a chair.

"Here is the back of the chair," she said.

Elsie walked around the chair and sat down. "Thank you," she said. She did not think she had ever been so happy to just sit down.

Shaylyn sat down in a creaky chair close to her. "You're welcome."

The school nurse's shoes squeaked as she walked out of her office. "Elsie, what's wrong? Oh, your knee is bleeding." She pulled another chair close to Elsie. "Put your foot up on this chair so I can look at your knee." Elsie put her foot up on the chair, and the nurse gasped. "Oh! This looks pretty bad."

"I tripped over something and fell," Elsie said.

"That looks worse than it did on the playground," Shaylyn said worriedly. "Will she need stitches?"

"She won't need stitches, but she will want to keep that bandaged for a couple days. I am going to roll up your pant leg so I can get a better look," the nurse warned. Elsie felt the jeans scrape across her hurt knee, and she winced. "I'm sorry," said the nurse, "I know that hurts. Were you with Elsie when she fell?" she asked Shaylyn.

"No, I wasn't with her. I was looking for dandelions, and then I saw Amy and Krista running away from her, and they dropped sticks."

While Shaylyn was talking, Mrs. Perry walked into the room.

"Amy and Krista?" she asked. Elsie could hear the frown in her voice. "They dropped sticks?"

Elsie sighed. "Yes. I played with them at recess. They said they wanted to show me their special spot. Amy said that it was a magical spot, and we had to run to get there before the portal closed. I tripped over something while we were running. I do not actually believe it was a portal, but I do not know what it was. When we got there, they told me to sit down, and they walked away. The next thing I knew something was scratching my arm and something else bounced off my forehead."

Mrs. Perry touched one of the scratches on Elsie's arm. "That explains the sticks, but what bounced off your forehead?"

Elsie heard the nurse open a package and smelled alcohol. Her knee burned when the nurse began to clean it. "Ouch!"

"I'm sorry I know that hurts," said the nurse.

Mrs. Perry asked, "Shaylyn, where was Elsie when you found her?"

"She was in the grass, a little way past the soccer field. She probably tripped on one of those tree stumps."

"Thank you. Now, you go to class, and I will sit with Elsie. On your way, would you tell Mrs. Conklin that Elsie and I are in the nurse's office?"

Shaylyn stood up. "Sure. I'll see you later, Elsie."

When Shaylyn left, Mrs. Perry sat down in the chair that Shaylyn had been sitting in.

"Something bounced off your forehead?" she asked gently.

Elsie reached into her pocket for the thing that had hit her. When she pulled it out, she could tell that it was a rock. Why hadn't she been able to tell what it was earlier? Mrs. Perry took the rock out of her hand.

"This is what they threw at you?"

"Yes, but I'm not sure why I put it in my pocket."

Mrs. Perry patted her hand. "I'm glad you did put it in your pocket. I am going to talk to the principal later, and I want to show her what they threw at you."

The nurse finished cleaning Elsie's knee; she put something on it that took the sting away and covered it with a bandage. "I'm going to gently roll down your pant leg," she said. "That bandage should hold until you get home. Let's have a look at the scratches on your arms." She picked up Elsie's left arm and examined it. "These scratches aren't deep. I'm going to clean them, but I don't think they need anything else."

"My hand hurts as well," Elsie said.

The nurse carefully looked at Elsie's hand. "You have a splinter. You must have accidentally put your hand on it when you fell over the tree stump."

Elsie heard the nurse open another alcohol wipe. "What will happen to Amy and Krista?" she asked as she felt the sting of the alcohol on her arm.

"The principal will talk with Amy and Krista's parents. They will also spend their recess in detention."

There was a lull in the conversation; the only sound in the room was the nurse opening a cabinet. Elsie liked the silence because it helped her think. She was hurt by what Amy and Krista had done to her. She wondered if they would blame her for their recess detention. Although she knew she could not be friends with them anymore, she still did not want them to hate her. It was hard to let go of the hope that they would ever include her.

Elsie was pulled away from her thoughts when the nurse walked back over. "I am going to have to pull that splinter out with tweezers," she said.

The nurse took Elsie's hand, and then there was a sharp pain. Mrs. Perry moved closer to Elsie and took her other hand.

"You can squeeze my hand if you need to," she offered.

Elsie sighed and squeezed Mrs. Perry's hand. "Amy and Krista were so nice to me at lunch. I thought that maybe they would finally be my friends. But they never wanted that."

Mrs. Perry patted Elsie's hand. "I'm sorry this happened to you. Shaylyn seems like a nice girl. Maybe you and she can become good friends."

"Shaylyn is nice," Elsie agreed. "I like sitting with her on the bus."

"I got the splinter out," the nurse announced, and wiped Elsie's hand with alcohol again.

"There are scratches on this arm too," Mrs. Perry said, and lifted Elsie's right arm for the nurse to see.

"They don't look deep," the nurse said as she inspected them. "I'll just clean them."

The butterflies in Elsie's stomach were still throwing a party. "My stomach kind of hurts," she said.

"After what you went through, I'm not surprised," Mrs. Perry said. "I have some peppermints in my purse; would you like one? That might help your stomach."

"Yes please," Elsie said. Mrs. Perry handed Elsie a peppermint, and she sucked on it. It did make her stomach feel a little better.

When the nurse finished cleaning Elsie's arm, Miss Perry stood up and said, "I am going to talk to the principal. Elsie, you should come with me. She will want to talk to you anyway, and this will keep you out of the classroom until the end of the day."

Elsie stood up to follow her; she was grateful that she would not have to go back to the classroom and face everyone. She knew she would have to see Amy and Krista eventually, but she was not ready yet.

At the principal's office, Mrs. Perry stopped to talk to the secretary, Mrs. Beck.

"Elsie! Mrs. Perry! How are you girls today?"

"Hi Mrs. Beck," said Mrs. Perry, "is Miss Lane in her office?"

"Yes. Do you need to talk to her?"

"Yes please. Right away, if possible."

"She's free right now, go on in."

Elsie wondered what Mrs. Beck was thinking. She had sounded so happy when she greeted them, but now her voice was sad. *Had she seen the scratches on her arms, or did she think Elsie was in trouble*? Elsie hated the idea that Mrs. Beck might think she was in trouble, but she also did not want Mrs. Beck feeling sorry for her if she saw the scratches on her arms. Her dad was always telling her that she should not care so much about what other people thought.

Elsie was pulled out of her thoughts when Miss Perry guided her the few steps to Miss Lane's office. They stopped while Mrs. Perry knocked on the door, and Miss. Lane's voice sounded muffled through the closed door when she said, "Come in."

Mrs. Perry led Elsie inside, and Miss Lane sounded surprised when she said, "Elsie, Mrs. Perry, what's wrong?" Mrs. Perry guided Elsie to a chair before she said anything, and Miss Lane kept talking. "Elsie? What happened? Did you get hurt?"

Elsie blinked back tears. She did not want to tell the story again, because each time she told the story, it made it truer. "Amy and Krista said they wanted to play with me at recess, so I went with them to their special spot." That was all she could get out before she had to stop and swallow, hard. She did not want to cry.

The principal put a hand on her arm. "Before you continue, let me call Mrs. Hill in. Is that okay with you?" Mrs. Hill was the school guidance counselor. She came into Elsie's class once a week to do a lesson, but Elsie did not know her very well. She had never talked with Mrs. Hill on her own before.

"Yes, that's fine."

Elsie heard Mrs. Lane dial a number on the phone and then ask, "Can you come to my office? I have a situation I could use your help with." A few minutes later, the door to Miss Lane's office opened and Elsie heard Mrs. Hill walk in.

"Elsie? Mrs. Perry? What is going on?" The counselor asked in surprise. "Elsie how did you get those scratches on your arm?"

Elsie hated that she would have to start her story all over again. Each time she told what Amy and Krista had done, she felt increasingly tired. She took a deep breath and let it out slowly before she spoke.

"Amy and Krista invited me to play with them at recess, they said they wanted to show me their special spot. When we got there—"

Mrs. Hill's hand on her arm interrupted her. "I'm sorry to stop you, but do you know where their special spot is?"

"Shaylyn said she found her past the soccer field," Mrs. Perry said.

"Past the soccer field? That is a long way out. Shaylyn is new here, isn't she? I remember working with her on the tests she had to take."

"Yes," Elsie said, "she is on my bus, and in my special reading class. I have been sitting with her."

"I am glad you are sitting with her. It can be hard to make new friends."

Miss Lane asked, "Was she with you, and Amy and Krista?"

"No, she didn't find me until after they left."

"They left?" Mrs. Hill's voice was surprised.

Elsie felt her shoulders tense up, and she was getting a headache. She rolled her shoulders, hoping it would take some of the knots out.

"When we got to their special spot, they told me to sit down. I had already tripped over a log because they said we had to run to get there."

Mrs. Hill touched her arm again. "Is that how you got the scratches on your arms?"

Elsie really wished Mrs. Hill would let her get through the story instead of interrupting her.

"No that's how I got a skinned knee." She started to talk faster, hoping she could get through her story quickly. "When I sat down, I felt them throw a rock at me." Something clattered on the table, and Elsie guessed it was the rock she had put in her pocket, and then given to Mrs. Perry. "For some reason I couldn't tell what it was at first, so I put it in my pocket." Elsie bit her lip and blinked back tears, and Mrs. Hill patted her hand.

"I got the scratches because they scratched me with sticks. At least, it was sticks. They tried to tell me that I stepped on a nest of monsters, and when I did not believe them, they said that the monsters were coming back, and they ran away. That is when Shaylyn found me."

"I told Elsie that they would spend their recess and lunch in detention," Mrs. Perry said.

Miss Lane's voice was angry as she agreed, "Yes, they will."

Mrs. Hill touched Elsie's arm again and asked, "Elsie, what would you like to happen?"

Elsie was silent for a minute. She had not really thought about what she would like to happen.

"I want to know why they did it," she finally said. "When they invited me to play with them, I thought they wanted to be my friends. I do not know why they would do this to me. And I also want to make sure they know what they did was wrong."

"I'm not sure they will tell you why they did it," Mrs. Hill said, "but they *will* spend their recesses in detention writing you apology letters. Also, they won't be allowed to go to the end-of-year picnic."

"We will also talk to their parents," Miss Lane added. "Our school has a zero-tolerance policy for bullying. I know those girls know better."

Elsie wondered what things would be like when they were out of detention. "How long will they be in detention?" she asked.

Mrs. Hill said, "I am not sure yet, but it will be a long time. Are you worried about what will happen when they get out of detention?"

"Yes, and I am also worried about what they will tell the girls in my class. No one wants to be friends with the class tattletale."

There was silence in the room for a minute and Elsie was worried. She wondered what the adults were thinking. Finally, Mrs. Perry said, "I do not think as many girls will believe them as you think. Yes, they are popular with a group of girls, but there are other girls that are quiet and keep to themselves."

"Can I sit with other people in class? I know that normally Mrs. Conklin does not normally change seating, but. . ."

Mrs. Hill put a hand on her arm and said, "Of course, we will move them, so you don't have to sit with them." Elsie felt relieved; she was thankful that she would not have to sit by Amy and Krista anymore. But just as she started to relax, Mrs. Hill continued, "We should call your parents as well, Elsie. We need to keep them informed on what is going on."

Elsie knew that she could not keep it from her parents. They would see the scratches and ask what happened. And she did not *want* to keep it from them, but right now she was too tired to talk about it anymore. She wondered what they would say when they were told. *Would they be mad at her for trying to be friends with Amy and Krista?*

"You should probably call my mom at her office. Neither of my parents are off work yet, but Mom's bosses will not care if she answers a personal call. Dad is probably still making deliveries."

"Okay. Do you want to stay for the conversation with your mom, or go to class?" Mrs. Hill asked.

Mrs. Perry said, "It is time for reading class. If you want, I will go to the classroom and get your book and pack up the rest of your things. That way, you do not have to see Amy and Krista again today, and their seats will be switched by tomorrow."

Elsie thought about it for a second. She liked sitting by Shaylyn and she guessed that Shaylyn was worried about her. She wanted to reassure Shaylyn that she was okay, and she liked the book they were reading. "I'll go to reading class," she decided.

"Tell Mr. Dean that I'll bring you your book, and I'll have the rest of your stuff in my office at the end of the day."

"Thank you. Will Mr. Dean think it is weird that you are bringing me my book?"

"He will probably just assume that I had to make some changes or something since I emboss all your books in my office. Do not worry, he will not think much about it."

Elsie felt better. She knew she had not done anything wrong, but she did not want Mr. Dean to ask what was going on because she was too tired to tell the story again. She stood up, ready to leave the office. "Thank you."

Elsie heard Mrs. Perry stand up too. "You're welcome." As they walked out, Miss Lane called after them, "Mrs. Perry, will you tell Mrs. Conklin to send Amy and Krista to the office?" Elsie had already started walking down the hallway, so she did not hear Mrs. Perry answer. She walked faster; she wanted to be safe in Mr. Dean's classroom before Amy and Krista came down the hall. When she got to Mr. Dean's room, she slumped into her chair and tried to smile at Shaylyn.

Shaylyn squeezed her hand in reply, and Elsie was thankful that she did not ask any questions.

Chapter 24
True Friends

That evening when Elsie got home, her dad asked to see her knee.

"The nurse is right," he said. "It looks bad, but it does not need stitches. Get a bath, and then I will bandage it."

Elsie hated putting her knee in the warm bath water. She was not sure what hurt worse: the pain in her heart, or her knee. When she got out of the bath, she went into the living room and sat down. Dad walked over and sat on the floor by her; he took her leg and put it in his lap so he could look at her knee.

"Is this the first time they've done this?" he asked,

Elsie felt her knee burn again as he cleaned it. "Yes. They haven't always been nice, but they never did anything like this."

Dad stopped wiping the alcohol wipe across her knee. "What do you mean they haven't always been nice?"

So, Elsie told him about the conversations she had with them when she got her cellphone, and when they were talking about the sleepover. She also told him what Krista said about Tanner taking her tray in the cafeteria.

Dad was quiet for a minute. "You know," he finally said, "I don't like you inviting yourself to other people's houses, but I hate that Amy's mom thinks you need more help than anyone else."

"I do need a little help getting around," Elsie said.

Dad dabbed something on her knee that took the sting away. "You need help knowing where things are, but you don't need help eating or anything like that. And that is what Amy's mom is thinking."

Elsie sighed. "I know it's not Amy's fault that her mom wouldn't want me at their house."

Dad opened a Band-Aid. "That's the *only* thing that isn't her fault," he growled. He smoothed the Band-Aid onto her skinned knee, put her foot down, and then looked at the scratches on her arms as he asked, "What do you think a true friend is?"

Elsie thought for a minute. "A true friend is someone who wants to be around you and enjoys spending time with you. Wouldn't a devoted friend try to explain to their mom that I do not need help eating or anything like that?"

"Yes," Dad agreed, "a devoted friend would try to explain to her mom what kind of help you do need. However, I do not think it is fair to blame Amy for what her mom thinks. People get ideas into their head and will not let them go no matter what other people tell them. Remember that Amy and Krista's families both think that you should be at the school for the blind."

Elsie had forgotten about that. She sat in silence while her dad got up and went in the kitchen to start supper. Elsie followed him into the kitchen so she could start her homework.

"I guess I haven't ever had a true friend," she said as she sat down at the table. She had never thought about it before, but now she realized she had spent so much time trying to get Amy and Krista to like her that she had not taken time to get to know the other girls in her class.

"What about Shaylyn?" Her dad asked as he sprayed cooking spray onto a baking pan.

"She's nice," Elsie said. "I do not know what would have happened if she had not found me. Mrs. Perry said that I should try to get to know her better. What are we having for dinner?" she asked as she heard Dad pour something onto the pan.

"We are having burgers and French fries. And Mrs. Perry is right, Shaylyn sounds like a nice girl. Don't push people away just because they're not the people you think you want to be friends with." He put the pan in the oven and walked out of the room; when he came back, he set Elsie's braille writer down in front of her.

"I don't think I've pushed Shaylyn away," she said, loading paper into her braille writer as Dad got her books out of her backpack.

"I didn't mean to say that you did," Dad said. "I just want you to make sure you *do not* push Shaylyn away. I know you don't know her very well, but from what you've told me about her, she sounds like a true friend."

Elsie thought about this. She decided that she would try to get to know Shaylyn better. After all, Shaylyn wanted to be her friend, and Amy and Krista did not. Elsie wondered why she had not noticed that before.

Later that night when she went to bed she prayed *Dear God, help me make some new friends, and help me be a good friend in return.*

Chapter 25
A New Kind of Friend

On Saturday, Elsie woke up early to the smell of pancakes and bacon. When she checked the time on her phone, it was only 7:00 AM. She walked into the kitchen and slumped into a chair at the table.

"Why are we eating so early?" she grumbled.

Dad set a plate down in front of her. "Your mom and I have a surprise for you, so you need to eat fast. We have to be there at eight."

When Elsie was finished eating, Mom said, "I put some clothes on your bed."

"Where are we going?" Elsie asked, but Mom only laughed.

"You'll find out when we get there."

Elsie found jeans, a T-shirt, and sweatshirt lying on her bed. She wondered where they were going. It could not be anywhere fancy, because these were clothes she would wear to school. They loaded up for a short drive, and then Dad announced, "We're here!"

Elsie got out of the car and took a few deep breaths. "It smells earthy here. Kind of like the barn at the fair."

Her dad laughed. "That would be horses you're smelling. Your mom and I decided to sign you up for horseback riding lessons."

Elsie walked with Dad through a gate, and she heard a horse neigh.

"Hi, you must be Elsie," a woman's voice called. "I am Elaine. Are you ready to ride?"

"Yes, I think so," Elsie said. "Mom and Dad kept it a surprise."

Elaine laughed. "Come on, we're going to put you on Cookie. She's very gentle." She led Elsie to the arena where she would be riding. "There's a stepstool right in front of you," she instructed. "You have three steps up."

Elsie reached out with her foot and felt the step. When she stepped up, someone took hold of her elbow.

"Hi Elsie, I'm Lilly," a new voice said. "I am going to be leading your horse today. My sister Laney is around here somewhere."

When Elsie had stepped up all three steps with Lilly's help, Elaine said, "Reach out in front of you, and you will feel Cookie. You can lean on her to help you get on." Elsie reached out and felt the saddle, and Elaine continued speaking. "If you lift your left foot up, you will feel the stirrup."

Elsie lifted her foot again and found the stirrup.

"That's good," Elaine encouraged. "Put your foot in the stirrup, lean on Cookie, and swing your right leg over her back."

Elsie swung her right leg over Cookie's back and found the other stirrup. And just like that, she had done it! She was on a horse!

Lilly said, "Good job, Elsie! Now, Elaine is going to walk beside you, and I am right beside you too. Do you want to learn how to make Cookie go?"

"Yes," Elsie said.

"Lilly, are you ready?" Elaine asked.

"I'm ready when you guys are," she answered.

"Ok Elsie," Elaine instructed, "kick your heels against Cookie's sides and make a click-click sound with your mouth, like this." Elaine made a clucking sound with her tongue, and Elsie kicked her heels against Cookie's sides and tried to imitate the same click-click sound with her mouth.

Cookie started moving, and Elsie felt amazed that she had made it happen. "I did it!" she exclaimed.

Elaine laughed. "Yes, you did it! Would you like to know what Cookie looks like?"

"Yes please," Elsie said.

"Cookie is a cherry sorrel mare. That means that she is a rich red. She has very expressive eyes. One is brown and one is half blue; it is not injured; it is just the way she is. She has a white star between her eyes, and a diamond of white on her nose. She also has some white on her lower lip, and three white feet."

"She's pretty," Elsie said.

While Elsie and Elaine were talking, Lilly led Cookie around the arena. Elsie loved the way it felt to be on top of a horse; it reminded her of being little and being carried piggy-back style by her dad.

"You're looking good up there. I don't think you even need me."

"I feel pretty good," said Elsie.

"You look like you've got your balance."

Elsie was confused when Cookie suddenly stopped walking. She tried kicking with her heels and "clicked" again with her mouth, but nothing happened. Elsie felt Cookie shift slightly, and then she heard what sounded like water being poured out of a bucket.

"Is she peeing?" she giggled.

Elaine and Lilly laughed too. Then Cookie moved again, and Elsie heard a soft "plop-plop" sound.

"Well, I know what that is," she said. "It stinks!"

Elaine and Lilly laughed again, and then Lilly yelled, "Laney! Come scoop the poop!"

Elsie heard footsteps, and then the scrape of a shovel on the ground. "Yay! Scooping poop is just what I wanted to do." Elsie laughed at that, and the new voice continued, "Hi Elsie, I'm Laney."

"Oh," Elsie was surprised. "You and Lilly sound just alike."

"No one around here can tell us apart," Laney said. "If you need somebody, just call either of us, and the closest one will answer."

When Laney finished scooping the poop, Elaine said, "Try to get her to go again."

Elsie kicked with her heels and clucked with her mouth. Cookie started to move forward, and Elsie said, "She's moving! It makes me feel good that she listens."

Elaine said, "Horses are good listeners. Can I be honest with you, Elsie? My horses are my best friends."

"Oh wow!" Elsie exclaimed. "That is cool. I don't have many friends."

"Would you like to get off a little early and just spend some time getting to know Cookie?" Elaine offered.

"Yes," Elsie agreed.

Elaine yelled, "Patrick, can you bring the steps over here?"

Elsie heard a "thump" as the stairs were set down beside them, and a voice said, "Hi Elsie, I'm Patrick. I am one of the horse trainers here. Lilly and Laney are the other trainers."

"Hi," she said,

Patrick told her, "Swing your right foot over Cookie's back, and bend your leg down. I'll help make sure your foot hits the step when you get off."

Lilly said, "I'm on the other side of you. I'll catch you if you fall."

"I'm here too," Elaine echoed. "Lean on Cookie to help you just like you did to get on."

Elsie leaned forward to put her weight on Cookie and swung her right foot over the horse's back. She was glad she had Cookie to lean on, because only having on foot in the stirrup was scary.

"You're doing great," Patrick said. "Bend your left leg and reach down with your right foot."

Elsie bent her left leg and moved her right foot down until she felt the step.

Patrick said, "You're doing well. You found the step. Pull your left leg out of the stirrup, and I'll help you come down the steps."

Elsie took her left foot out of the stirrup and felt his hand on her elbow. "You're going to come down the stairs backwards," he told her.

After Patrick and Lilly helped her down the stairs, Lilly asked "Would you like to pet Cookie for a little bit?"

"Yes please," Elsie said.

"I'll tie her up," Lilly said as she led Cookie away.

Elaine bumped Elsie's elbow and said, "I'll lead you to where Cookie is going to be tied up."

Elsie took Elaine's arm, and they walked across the arena. When they reached Lilly and Cookie, Elaine took Elsie's hand and put it on the horse.

"She's so soft," Elsie said.

"If you move to your left a little bit, you'll be by her head."

Elsie moved to her left and touched Cookie's cheek. She stroked down the horse's soft cheek to her neck. Cookie shifted her weight and rested her head on Elsie's shoulder.

"She must like you," said Elaine. "She doesn't rest her head on just anyone's shoulder."

"I'm glad she likes me."

Elaine moved closer to Elsie and whispered, "When your dad signed you up for lessons, he told me about what happened on the playground."

Elsie pressed her cheek against Cookie's neck and blinked back tears. "I don't understand why they did it."

"There's no good answer," said Elaine, "but the best answer I can give you is, they're not nice, and probably a little insecure."

Elsie inhaled Cookie's scent. "But they're the most popular girls in school. What do they have to be insecure about?"

Elaine patted Elsie's shoulder. "You never know what's on the inside of someone. Just because they're the most popular girls in school doesn't mean they don't have issues of their own."

Elsie sighed. "I never thought about that. I wanted to be friends with them because they are popular. But there is another girl at school who is nicer to me. I think I should get to know her better."

"I think that's a good idea," Elaine agreed.

"Are you ready to go, sissy?" her dad interrupted them.

"How long have you been here?" she asked.

"I stayed to watch you ride," he said. "I took some pictures and sent them to your mom. Did you have fun?"

"Yes, I had fun. Cookie is a nice horse."

"We'll have her steering Cookie herself in a few weeks," said Lilly.

"Good deal," Elsie's dad said.

Elaine patted Elsie's shoulder. "Schedule your next ride with Kathy before you leave. She's in the office."

"See you next week," Elsie called.

Lilly and Laney both said, "Bye Elsie! It was nice to meet you. We will see you next week!"

"Bye," Elsie waved. "See you all next week."

Chapter 26
A New Friend Group

The next day at lunch, Elsie wondered who Mrs. Lester would tell her to sit by. She also wondered if Mrs. Lester had heard the whole story about what Amy and Krista had done. *If Mrs. Lester had heard what happened, was she mad at Elsie for not telling her the whole truth?* Elsie thought Mrs. Lester seemed quieter than usual when she met her in the cafeteria.

The teacher asked, "Who would you like to sit with since Tanner isn't here?" Tanner was still out sick; Elsie hoped he would get better soon, because she missed talking to him before school and at lunch.

"I don't know who to sit with," she admitted. She was afraid of what Amy and Krista might have been saying about her. *What might the other girls in her class think of her now?*

"Why don't you sit with Marie?"

"Okay," Elsie agreed, "but I don't know Marie very well."

"She's very shy and quiet, but she is a nice girl."

Elsie sat nervously at the table and wondered what Marie might have heard about her from Amy and Krista. *What if Marie thought she was a tattletale who had just wanted to get Amy and Krista in trouble? What if she would not talk to her?*

Elsie was startled to feel a light touch on her arm, and a voice said, "Hi, I am Marie. I have not talked to you much because you always sit with Tanner, or Amy and Krista, but I have wanted to talk to you. I sit close to you in class now."

Elsie felt relieved that Marie had talked to her, because she was too nervous to try and start a conversation herself. "Hi, Marie. I was wondering who was sitting beside me now but there was not time to ask this morning."

"I'm beside you now, and I think they are going to put Brandon beside us, but he's out sick today."

"Tanner is too. It seems like something is going around."

"I had strep throat last week," Marie said. "I guess I could have accidentally given it to Brandon."

"I'm glad I haven't gotten it yet."

"You are lucky. It seems to be making its way through the class, but maybe you will be the lucky one who does not get it."

"I hope so," Elsie wished. They were silent for a second, and Elsie took a bite of her burger. She did not know what to talk about.

Finally, Marie asked, "Do you know why they had Brandon and I switch seats with Amy and Krista?"

Elsie was afraid to say the wrong thing. She took her time chewing her burger before she finally answered, "They weren't very nice to me."

"Oh, I'm not surprised," Marie said. "They aren't nice girls."

Elsie was shocked; she had *never* heard anyone say anything like that about Amy and Krista. "You don't think they are nice?"

"No. They make you think they are nice, but they are not. Last year, Amy was in my class, and she invited all the kids in our class to her birthday party. Krista was there because even though she was not in class with us, she and Amy have been friends for years."

"Krista was in my class last year. What did you guys do at the party? I do not think Amy had one this year. If she did, she did not invite the whole class."

"Her family rented the indoor swimming pool. They had to rent the indoor one because her birthday is in December."

"That sounds like fun," Elsie said, a little enviously.

"It wasn't!" Marie's voice was angry.

"What happened?" Elsie asked in surprise.

"I went through a growth spurt last fall, so I did not have a swimsuit to wear, and you cannot find them in stores in December. Mom had to get one online and the only one she could find in my size was an ugly green one. They called me "green bean" for the rest of the year. I am tall, by the way; I was not sure if you knew that."

Elsie felt bad for Marie, but in a strange way it made her feel better to know that she was not the only one that Amy and Krista bullied. "I didn't know that" she said. "I don't think I've ever walked with you."

"Maybe I can sit with you in the morning, and help you get out of the gym," Marie suggested.

"I would like that," Elsie smiled.

*

When it was time for recess, Shaylyn came over to Elsie and asked, "Do you want to come hang out with me and my friends?"

"Sure," Elsie agreed.

Marie said quietly, "I'll see you in class, Elsie."

Elsie was surprised at how sad Marie sounded. She leaned close to Shaylyn and whispered, "Can Marie come too?"

Shaylyn immediately said, "Marie, do you want to come hangs out with us in the playhouse?"

"Will the others mind?" Marie sounded nervous.

"Hannah and Zoe won't mind," Shaylyn promised. "Besides, it's cold outside today, so the more people we get in the little playhouse, the warmer it will be."

Once all the girls were crammed into the playhouse, Shaylyn said, "Hannah, Zoe, this is Elsie and Marie."

"Hi Elsie," Zoe said, "I don't know if you remember, but we were in first grade together."

"Oh, okay," Elsie said.

Hannah added, "We haven't been in any classes together, but I was an elf with you in the Christmas play."

"Were you the one who helped me?" Elsie remembered.

"Yes."

"It's nice to actually meet you," Elsie smiled. "I don't think I learned your name during the program."

"It's okay," Hannah said.

Marie said, "I think I've had both of you in my class before."

Hannah asked the group, "What do you guys think about having to switch classes next year?"

Elsie said, "I am not looking forward to carrying a bunch of books around. I know we have lockers, but it would be hard to go to your locker after each class."

"My sister says we only have four minutes between classes," Hannah said.

Shaylyn laughed. "That will be hard for you because you like to talk."

Everyone joined Shaylyn and Hannah in a laugh, and then Hannah agreed, "Yes, I do like to talk, but Elsie's right; it would be hard to go back to your locker after each class. My sister is in eighth grade now, and she says she goes to her locker before school and gets what she needs for her before lunch classes. She does not go to her locker again until lunch time."

Marie said, "That does sound hard. I do not think I want to carry all those textbooks around. Elsie, your books are even bigger than ours, what will you do?"

Elsie was happy to be included. "I do not know. I will have to get a big backpack."

"Why are your books bigger than ours?" Hannah asked.

"Braille books are bigger than print books; the bumps take up more room."

Zoe said, "I remember seeing the bumps in first grade and thinking they were cool."

"I think braille looks cool too," Shaylyn echoed. "It's cool to watch you read in reading class."

"I hate reading out loud," Elsie admitted. "I'm always afraid I'm going to be the slowest." Elsie prayed that Marie did not say anything about her reading upside-down, but the other girl surprised her when she said,

"I don't think you read super slow."

Shaylyn touched Elsie's arm and said, "I don't think you do either."

"I hope we don't have to read out loud in middle school," Elsie said.

Shaylyn giggled. "That would be something to look forward to."

Hannah said, "I am not looking forward to all the homework, but I am looking forward to all the fun things we get to do in middle school. I cannot be a cheerleader, until seventh grade, but I am going to join the pep squad."

"What's the pep squad?" Elsie asked.

"You sit in the stands during all the home games and do the cheers with the cheerleaders, so people learn them. You also must help make posters and banners."

Shaylyn said, "That sounds boring. Besides, it will be cold at the games, and I hate being cold. It is cold now; I hope recess is over soon."

Elsie scooted closer to Shaylyn, and Shaylyn put an arm around her shoulders. Elsie wrapped her arm around Shaylyn's waist and was surprised when she felt someone come to stand on her other side and wrap an arm around her shoulder.

Zoe said, "Elsie has the right idea! Let us all get closer for warmth."

Elsie wrapped her other arm around Zoe, and soon she could tell that Hannah and Marie had joined the huddle as well.

Zoe said, "I've heard we don't get a recess in middle school, so I guess we should enjoy it now."

Hannah agreed. "My sister said she gets a little break after lunch, but there isn't a playground."

"I'll miss swinging," Elsie said, a little sadly.

"I swing beside you sometimes," Zoe said, "but I never know what to say to you."

"I sometimes wonder who is swinging near me, especially when I'm not with a friend."

Marie said, "I was over there that day Amy and Krista were swinging with you. I wanted to say something after they went to jump rope, but I did not know what to say either."

"I want to know who's around me," Elsie said, "but I am afraid that I will ask who is around and there will not be anyone there. Then I will be the crazy girl that talks to herself." The others laughed, and Elsie realized that this was what Mrs. Perry meant when she said that her devoted friends would laugh *with* her, not at her.

She jumped when the end-of-recess whistle blew and interrupted her thoughts.

"I was just starting to kind of get warm," Shaylyn complained.

Elsie laughed and said, "Me too."

Zoe stayed close to Elsie and said, "Hey, let's walk huddled up like this until we get to our class lines."

They all laughed as they walked out of the playhouse, moving slowly in an effort not to step on each other's feet. When they reached the blacktop where the classes were lining up, Marie said, "Elsie, can I help you line up with our class?"

"Sure," Elsie said, and shivered as their group separated.

"It's going to be cold again tomorrow," Hannah said. "We should do that again."

Marie asked, "Can I join you guys again?"

"You and Elsie are both invited," said Hannah.

Elsie felt someone bump her with their elbow and she guessed it was Marie. She took Marie's arm and as they walked away together Marie leaned close and said, "Thanks for asking if I could join you."

Elsie felt both happy and surprised. *Had she just helped someone else feel included?* Usually, *she* was the one hoping someone else would include her. "You're welcome," she said. "You sounded so sad, and I didn't want you to feel left out."

"Thank you," Marie squeezed her arm. "It's always been hard for me to make friends, and since I grew so tall last year, I guess I feel really awkward."

"I like walking with people who are taller than me. I feel a bit more secure walking with taller people."

"That makes sense," Marie said.

As their class left the cold playground and walked inside, Elsie wondered, *Is this what it feels like to have a friend group?*

Chapter 27
Preparing for Valentine's Day

A few weeks had gone by, and it was now the night before Valentine's Day. Elsie, her mom, dad, and little brother were preparing Valentine's Day goodie bags for Elsie's class and the kids at day care.

"Mommy, can I have a piece of candy?" said Blake.

Elsie heard her mom crack her knuckles; she knew her mom did that when she was at the end of her rope. Blake just could not understand that the candy was not for him to eat now, but to give away tomorrow, and he kept asking for treats. Mom sounded irritated and tired when she said, "No, you may not have any candy," and kept stuffing Hershey's kisses into little plastic bags with hearts on them.

While Mom and Blake put candy in bags, Elsie brailed "Happy Valentine's Day" on cards; her dad took the cards from her and wrote out with a marker what she had brailled on them before stapling them to the bags.

"How come Elsie is brailling the ones for Linda's house as well as the ones for her class?" Blake asked.

Elsie took a card out of the braille writer and handed it to her dad. She grabbed another card from the pile in front of her and put it into the braille writer.

"Don't you think the kids at Linda's house would like to feel the braille?" Dad asked as he finished writing on the card and stapled it to one of the bags.

"I guess so," Blake said. "It does feel cool. The bumps are fun to run your hand across." Blake put a sucker in the bag and passed it to his mom, who put two Hershey's kisses into the bag.

"We kind of have an assembly line going," Elsie said as she took the next card out of the braille writer and handed it to her dad. She loved doing things like this with her family.

"Yes, we do," Dad agreed. He stapled the card to the bag Mom handed him and set it on the pile of finished bags.

"Since Elsie and I are both working on all the bags, does that mean we have to share all the candy?" Blake asked.

Mom and Dad were silent for a minute. Elsie wondered if they had thought about that yet. At Halloween they had shared the candy, but they had more candy then. Blake had gotten candy at Linda's house, and Elsie had gotten candy at school. Then they went trick-or-treating and had even more candy. They had still been eating Halloween candy at Thanksgiving, and there had been enough candy that they had not had to fight over their favorites.

This time would be different, Elsie would have more candy because there were more kids in her class than there were at Linda's house. If Elsie had to share her Valentine's candy with Blake, he would take all the good stuff. They both preferred the fun-sized chocolate candy bars, and they particularly fought over KitKat, because KitKat was their favorite.

Over the past few years, Elsie had noticed that at Halloween, most people gave out fun-sized candy bars, but on Valentine's, most people got heart-shaped suckers and conversation hearts. Elsie and Blake would eat the suckers, but neither one liked the conversation hearts, so their dad ate the ones they got. This left them with less candy to split between them.

Elsie knew that she had a better chance of getting chocolate than Blake did. She guessed that a lot of kids at Linda's house would bring suckers because parents could watch the little ones with suckers and make sure they did not choke. If Blake did not get any chocolate, but Elsie did, Blake would expect her to share all the chocolate she got. She guessed she did not mind sharing with Blake, but she knew that if she did not go through her candy before she shared it with him, he would grab the KitKat before she knew she had any.

"I don't mind sharing with Blake," she said. "How about we both go through our own candy and pick out our favorites, and then we can share the rest."

Blake started to cry. "I don't want to share my candy!"

"Well, I don't really want to share my candy with you either!" Elsie felt bad as soon as the words were out of her mouth. *Why had she said anything?* She knew that it was getting to be past Blake's bedtime, and he was tired.

Blake started to wail. "But you will have more candy! I will not have as much as you, so I should not have to share!"

Elsie felt bad because now she had made things worse. "I'm sorry," she said.

Mom sighed. "Come on, Blake. It's time for bed."

"But I haven't finished yet!" he argued.

"If you don't do what your mother says and go to bed right now, you won't get any candy tomorrow!" Dad said.

Blake was still crying when Mom carried him to bed. Elsie handed another card to her dad.

"I'm sorry," she said. "I did not mean it. I do not mind sharing with him. I know I will have more than him."

Elsie's dad sighed. "You have to learn not to let the things your brother says get to you. He is younger than you and does not understand sharing very well yet. You need to lead by example."

"I know, I'm sorry," she said again.

"Then go get ready for bed. Your mom and I will finish getting them ready. We will have extra candy left over, so Blake can have that. He will be so excited tomorrow; he will not even remember crying tonight."

Elsie went to the bathroom and brushed her teeth. She then went into her bedroom, put on her pajamas, and got into bed. Her stuffed bunny was waiting for her on her pillow. Elsie wondered if her dad would give her a stuffed animal for Valentine's Day this year. He usually gave her a teddy bear or a puppy.

When her mom and dad were finished with the bags, they came into tuck Elsie into bed and say good night. Elsie drifted off to sleep wondering about what good things might happen tomorrow.

Chapter 28
Will You Be My Valentine?

When Elsie got to school the next morning, Mrs. Lester sat her by Tanner.

Elsie smiled and said, "Hi, Tanner. How are you?"

"I'm good," he said.

She took her backpack off and held it in her lap. It was much heavier today with all the goodie bags inside. "Are you ready for the Valentine's Day party?" she asked.

Tanner was silent for a second. "It will be nice to not have to do our afternoon classes," he finally said.

"I hope we don't have any homework today," she answered.

Elsie heard Tanner scoot closer to her. "I want to ask you a question." Elsie turned toward him, concerned; he sounded serious. "Will you . . . um, will you . . . be my girlfriend?"

Elsie wanted to squeal with happiness. She had daydreamed about this, but she had not thought it would happen.

"Yes, I would love to be your girlfriend," she said. But she did not know what to say next. *Was it too soon to ask him to go with her to the end-of-year dance*? She really wanted him to ask her. *What should she say now*? She had wanted him to ask her to be his girlfriend, but now she did not know what to do. Her daydreams had only gone as far as him asking her the question.

In her daydreams, romantic music had played in the background. Elsie knew that in real life there would not be any romantic music playing, but she wished that something else would happen, or one of them would think of something to say.

Finally, Tanner touched her shoulder. "What do we do now that we are boyfriend and girlfriend?"

"I don't know," Elsie said, not sure what else to say. "We do what we have already been doing; we walk together and sit together at lunch. I can give you my phone number if you want."

Elsie heard Tanner unzip his backpack, and he said, "I bring my phone to school. I know we are not supposed to, but my mom likes me to have it. You can give me your number now if you want." Elsie recited her phone number for him, and he continued, "I'll text you later tonight, so you have my number too. I remember you saying you could text."

Elsie was happy that he remembered something so small. She heard him put his phone back in his backpack, and she wondered if he had brought any Valentine's Day candy. She wondered what he would do while they all handed out candy if he had not brought anything.

They sat in silence until the bell rang. When their grade was dismissed, Tanner walked with her to class. While she was on her way to her seat, she heard Mrs. Conklin walk over to Tanner. Elsie heard the teacher whisper,

"I brought some suckers for you to pass out during the party. I didn't want you to feel left out."

Elsie did not think anyone else had heard Mrs. Conklin, but she was surprised when Tanner said "Thanks, Mrs. Conklin." Elsie was surprised that he sounded so happy. After the talk she and her dad had during the can drive, Elsie thought that Tanner would be mad that Mrs. Conklin had brought suckers for him to pass out. She wondered if Mrs. Conklin, or her dad, was right. *Could they both be right?*

At that moment, it did not matter who was right. She was simply happy that her boyfriend would not be left out today. Elsie loved being able to call Tanner her boyfriend.

*

When Elsie had unpacked her backpack, she took last night's homework to Mrs. Perry.

"Happy Valentine's Day," she said as she handed the stack of paper to Mrs. Perry. "Here is last night's homework."

"Happy Valentine's Day to you too," Mrs. Perry said, and handed her a work sheet. "This is a Valentine's word search puzzle Mrs. Conklin has for the class to do."

"Oh, okay." Elsie took the worksheet to her desk, and then walked her backpack out to her locker. When she got back in the classroom, she sighed and got to work. She *hated* word searches. A frown spread across her face as she wondered if teachers thought kids liked holiday-themed word puzzles, or did they give them the word puzzles so they could get some learning done before the party?

Elsie had always hated word searches. She was not sure how the other kids did word searches, but she thought they circled the different letters for each word. Elsie was stuck just writing them on her braille writer. It was complicated for her, because the scrambled letters were on one page, and the words she was looking for were on a second page. Elsie hated when she was looking for a word that she did not know how to spell very well. She had to keep flipping pages so she could remember how the word was spelled.

She would never actually do it, but every time she did a word search puzzle, she thought about cheating. *After all, who would know that she had not actually looked through the scrambled letters to find the word?* But Mrs. Perry might be able to tell, and if she noticed what Elsie was doing, she would tell Mrs. Conklin. Elsie hated when Mrs. Perry and Mrs. Conklin were mad at her.

She loaded a piece of paper into the braille writer. The first thing on the work sheet was the page of scrambled letters: **v c k l o a h i u l o s e e c s t l s l a i a n t e e**

Elsie turned to the next page and saw that the words she was looking for were "chocolate," "kiss," "love," and "Valentines." She thought she could see the word "love" easily. Once Elsie finished finding the letters for "love" and writing them on her paper, she decided to tackle "kiss" next. She knew that "chocolate" and "Valentines" would be harder because she would have to flip the page to keep looking at the spelling.

She wished she could crack her knuckles like her mom did when she was frustrated. Mom had tried to show her how to do it once, but Elsie was afraid it would hurt and so she decided not to try.

As she worked on the word search, Elsie thought about the clock on the wall. She knew there was a clock in the classroom because when the room was quiet, she could hear it ticking. She could not hear it today because everyone was so loud, but she imagined it; she imagined that it was going extra slow on purpose, just to keep them from the party. She thought she could hear it ticking extra slowly: tick . . . tick . . . tick . . . tick. . .

As the day wore on, Elsie decided that it was not just the clock in the classroom that was going slowly; *all* the clocks in the entire school must be dragging. She wondered if the teachers had purposefully made all the clocks go slower.

Finally, it was time for the party. Mrs. Perry walked over to Elsie and said, "I am going to put the braille writer on my desk so that the icing and sprinkles from the cupcakes do not get on it. Mrs. Conklin has brought cupcakes with red and pink sprinkles, and heart-shaped rings on top."

"Okay thank you," Elsie said.

When Mrs. Perry was gone, Marie walked over and said, "I'm putting a pink napkin on your desk."

"Thank you." Elsie unfolded her napkin so that it would hopefully catch all the crumbs. She could tell when Mrs. Conklin was at her desk because she could smell the cupcakes. She took a big sniff; she always loved the scent of vanilla, but she thought there was something especially magical about the scent of vanilla on a holiday.

"Elsie, would you like a chocolate or white cupcake?"

"Chocolate, please."

"It's right in front of you," the teacher told her.

"Thank you," Elsie said, and felt cautiously in front of her. She took the ring off the top of her cupcake and licked off the frosting before setting it on her napkin. She was careful when she took the cupcake out of the paper; she hated it when cupcakes fell apart. She took a bite of the cupcake, and the taste of chocolate and buttercream frosting exploded on her tongue.

When she was finished, she tried to make sure that all the crumbs were wrapped up in her napkin as she gathered it up.

"Don't throw your ring away," Marie reminded her.

"Thank you. I almost forgot it was there."

Elsie set the ring down on her desk and went to throw the napkin away. When she got back to her desk, Mrs. Perry was waiting to help her pass out her goodie bags. They walked to each student and Elsie handed them a goodie bag and told them "Happy Valentine's Day."

Many of the kids in her class were excited to get their cards. "Cool! I have braille of my own now!" one student exclaimed.

And another said, "Thanks Elsie! I love feeling the bumps!"

Mom was right, Elsie thought, the kids *did* love feeling the braille. She was happy that she had put braille on her cards. It made her goodie bags different than all the others. Elsie even had goodie bags for Mrs. Conklin and Mrs. Perry; she had made sure her mom had enough for the teachers, too.

When she got back to her desk, she started organizing the cards and candy she had gotten so far. She was happy she had the bag that had held her goodie bags to load up with the new cards and candy. As she put things in her bag, she looked at the kind of candy she got. *Was that a KitKat?* She was tempted to eat it right away so she would not have to fight Blake for it. He would cry if he saw the KitKat. But Mrs. Conklin had told their class that if she saw anyone eating candy in the classroom, she would take it away.

Elsie held the KitKat longingly for a second, and then put it in the bag with the other candy. Someone handed out Sweet Tarts next. Elsie hated Sweet Tarts but put them in her bag anyway; she would give them to her dad because she knew he loved them.

While the last person handed out their candy, Elsie heard a cart rolling down the hallway and into the classroom.

"Hi Mrs. Conklin," an unfamiliar voice said, "I have deliveries for a few of your students." Elsie wondered whose parents had things delivered to the school for them. She was surprised when a fuzzy teddy bear was set down on her desk. She reached out and stroked its soft head, and Mrs. Perry walked over.

"Oh, that is so cute," she said. "It's a white bear, with pink hearts on its paws." She took Elsie's hand and put it on the heart on the bear's paw. Mrs. Perry stroked the teddy bear too. "It's soft, too. It has a card tied to it. Would you like me to read it to you?"

"Yes please," Elsie said, and heard Mrs. Perry open the card.

"*Dear Elsie,*" she read aloud, "*we hope you are having a happy Valentine's Day. Love, Mom and Dad.*"

Elsie hugged the teddy bear tight. "Dad usually gets me something for Valentine's Day, but he's never had it delivered to the school before!"

"The students with gifts from their families need to take them to their lockers until the end of the day," Mrs. Conklin announced. Elsie sighed and stood up. She held the teddy bear under her arm, grabbed her cane, and walked out to her locker. She had wanted to keep her bear with her for the rest of the day, and she wondered why Mrs. Conklin had to take the fun out of everything.

When she got back in the classroom, she heard Mrs. Conklin trying to get everyone to settle down. "Boys and girls," she said, "*boys and girls*! If you do not settle down, you will not hear the announcement I have. And I think you would all be sad if you missed this."

The classroom got so quiet that Elsie could hear the clock ticking. "As a Valentine's gift to you," Mrs. Conklin continued, "I have decided that you don't have to do your reading tonight."

Many of the kids cheered at that. "Yay! No homework!"

After that, the end-of-school bell rang, and Elsie went out to her locker to get her backpack. She quickly shoved the teddy bear inside, and then walked back into the classroom and put her bag of candy in beside the teddy. She did not need to worry about her homework folder because there was no homework. She decided to leave her books in her desk; it would make her load much lighter.

Now that the party was over, Elsie was almost sad. Aside from the word search puzzle, it had been an enjoyable day. Tanner had asked her to be his girlfriend in the morning, and they had the party, and she had gotten a teddy bear in the afternoon. She wished that the clocks had kept ticking slowly; it seemed as if, once they got to the good part of the day, someone sped the clocks up, so they went at super-speed.

She did not stay sad for long because she realized that Valentine's Day was on Wednesday this year. Elsie could enjoy choir and midweek without worrying about homework! That did not happen very often, so she was excited to be able to enjoy choir and midweek without rushing home to finish homework. She wondered, what they would be doing at midweek today.

She jumped when she felt a hand on her shoulder. Tanner said, "I'm sorry I just wanted to tell you that . . . um, I'm glad you're my girlfriend, and I'll text you later, so you have my number."

"Okay," Elsie said, feeling both excited and shy. As she grabbed her backpack, she wondered how Shaylyn's day had been. Elsie could not wait to ask Shaylyn about how her party had gone. She wondered if Shaylyn's family got her anything for Valentine's Day.

Chapter 29
Best Friends

When Elsie was ready to go, she walked to the bus loading area and met Shaylyn. Mrs. Perry never came with her to the bus area anymore unless Shaylyn was sick. Shaylyn liked helping Elsie get on the bus. "Hi Elsie, how was your afternoon?" she asked.

"It was good," Elsie answered with a smile.

"Yeah, it must have been a good day. You got a boyfriend in the morning, and then had a Valentine's party this afternoon." Elsie had told Shaylyn about Tanner asking her to be his girlfriend at recess that morning, and Shaylyn had been just as excited as Elsie was.

"When we get on the bus, I want to show you what my dad got me," Elsie said. She did not know why, but she was not afraid to show Shaylyn the teddy bear. She would *never* have shown the teddy bear to Amy and Krista.

"My dad got me something too. Can I show you what I got?" Shaylyn asked. She sounded nervous, and Elsie wondered why.

"Sure, I would love to see what your parents sent you," she said.

When they got on the bus, Elsie, and Shaylyn both took off their backpacks. "Let's wait until everyone is sitting down to show each other what we got," Shaylyn whispered. "I'll tell you when the coast is clear."

Elsie laughed at that. "Okay."

Once the bus started moving, Shaylyn said "Okay, the coast is clear now."

Elsie laughed again. "It sounds like we're planning some secret operation." Shaylyn laughed too, and both girls unzipped their back packs. Elsie reached into her backpack to pull out the teddy, but then realized that the bear was kind of large and would probably attract attention. "It's kind of big, and I'm afraid to get it out, but look in my pack. Isn't it cute?" Elsie handed Shaylyn her backpack.

"Oh, it's so cute and soft!" Shaylyn exclaimed.

"Mrs. Perry told me that it's white, with pink hearts on the paws."

"Yes, and it has pink buttons for eyes," Shaylyn said. "Did you feel the nose? It is heart-shaped too. Can I show you?"

"Sure," Elsie agreed. She was glad that Shaylyn had asked instead of just grabbing her hand. Shaylyn took her hand and put it on the teddy bear's nose.

"That's so cool," Elsie said as she felt it. "The nose is in the shape of a heart, and it is soft." Elsie zipped up her backpack again and put it under her seat. "Can I see what you got?"

Shaylyn handed her a stuffed animal that was smaller than Elsie's teddy bear. "It's a brown puppy. The ears are heart-shaped, and it has a pink flower in its mouth instead of a bone." Elsie felt the dog's face to find the flower in its mouth, and then felt the heart-shaped ears. Elsie liked the ears. She did not think Shaylyn's puppy was as soft as her bear, but she would not say that to her friend.

"It's so small and cute," Elsie said as she handed the puppy back to Shaylyn, and Shaylyn put it in her backpack.

"I love stuffed animals," Shaylyn said. "I was afraid to show you my puppy until I saw your teddy bear. I am going to name my puppy Rosie because the flower in her mouth looks like a rose. What are you going to name your teddy bear?"

"I think I might name her Annabel," Elsie said.

"That's a good name," Shaylyn agreed. They were quiet for a minute, and Shaylyn was rubbing her hands together.

"Are you okay?" Elsie asked. "You're rubbing your hands together, and I've noticed you do that when you are nervous."

Shaylyn sighed. "I'm sorry, I don't always realize when I'm doing it."

"It doesn't bother me," Elsie told her. "I just wanted to make sure you were okay."

"I wanted to ask you if maybe we could be best friends," Shaylyn said after another moment of quiet. "Hannah and Zoe are nice, but sometimes they are hard to talk to. They've been best friends for years, and sometimes I kind of feel left out."

Elsie remembered what her dad said after she had been hurt by Amy and Krista. "I don't have a best friend. I used to think that Amy and Krista would be my best friends, but I learned that they are not very nice."

Shaylyn stopped rubbing her hands together. "We can be best friends?" She sounded both nervous and hopeful.

"It will be nice to have a best friend," Elsie agreed. "I've never had one before."

They sat in silence for a few minutes after that. Elsie wanted to ask Shaylyn for her phone number but was worried that Shaylyn would be like Amy and not want to text her because she could not see pictures. But then she remembered that Tanner had been happy to take her number, and he had said he would text her later. *What if he never texted her*?

Her thoughts were going round and round like the clothes in the washing machine, and Elsie did not know what to do. Finally, Shaylyn broke the silence.

"Can I have your number? Maybe we could talk on the phone some time."

"I would like that," Elsie said. "If you text, I can text as well." She felt a sense of relief, and her thoughts stopped tumbling around like the clothes in the washing machine. It was hard for her to always be the one to take the initiative. She hated trying to guess whether a person would want to take her number or not, and she was thankful that Shaylyn asked for her number.

"That's cool," Shaylyn said. "How does it work?"

"My phone talks to me. I will show you sometime. My mom doesn't let me take my phone to school."

Elsie heard Shaylyn unzip her backpack. "My mom wants me to take my phone just in case of an emergency. Let me create a new contact." Elsie waited while Shaylyn created a new contact. "Turn toward me so I can take a picture of you to put with your contact info." Elsie turned toward Shaylyn and heard her taking a photo. Elsie loved the "camera" sound phones made when they took a picture. "Okay. What is your number?" Shaylyn asked.

Elsie gave Shaylyn her number.

"Got it," the other girl said. "Can I take a picture of us together?"

"Sure," Elsie smiled. She leaned in close to Shaylyn, and Shaylyn took a picture. "I'll text you later. Would you like me to send you the picture?"

"Yes please!" Elsie said. "Are you on Facebook?"

"Yes, I'm on Facebook. Are you?"

"Yes."

"I'll friend you!" Shaylyn exclaimed. She had just put her phone back in her backpack when the bus stopped at her stop. She quickly hugged Elsie before she left and said, "I'm glad we're friends."

After Shaylyn was gone, Elsie realized that none of her friends had ever given her a hug before. She wondered, why not. Elsie had always liked hugs, so getting one from Shaylyn seemed extra special. Hugs made Elsie feel safe and happy. After what happened with Amy and Krista, Elsie was glad to feel a sense of safety with Shaylyn.

Buzzing with excitement, Elsie leaned her head back against the seat. She now had a boyfriend, a best friend, and a horse friend. *What was in store for her next?*

Ritz Chicken Recipe

Ingredients:

Two pounds boneless skinless chicken breasts, cut into large strips.
Two sleeves Ritz crackers, crushed into fine crumbs.
One stick of salted butter, melted.
Salt and pepper to taste

Steps:

Preheat oven to 350 degrees. Season chicken strips with salt and pepper if desired. Working one at a time, dip each chicken strip into the melted butter, and then roll in cracker crumbs and place on a greased baking sheet. Bake the chicken for approx. 45 minutes, until the strips are golden brown, and the chicken has reached an internal temperature.

Tomato Rice Recipe

Ingredients:

2 cups quick-cooking rice such as Minute Rice (Note: this recipe will not work with traditional or brown rice)
2 cups chicken broth
2 8-ounce cans of unseasoned tomato sauce
Salt and pepper to taste

Steps:

Bring chicken broth to a boil in medium-sized pot. Add two cups rice to the pot, and remove from heat; cover with lid, and let sit for five minutes until rice has absorbed all liquid. Stir in both cans of tomato sauce, season with salt and pepper if desired, and serve immediately with Ritz chicken.

About the Author

BRECK CAMPBELL is a native of Boonville, MO. She was the first child to parents that had no idea what they were doing. They do not give instruction manuals. Breck was born with Septo-Optic Dysplasia and had absolutely no vision since birth. This disability created challenges and struggles for Breck however you would never know by the smile on her face. Breck never let her diagnosis hinder her spirit or her desire to succeed, it did however, often leave her as an outsider. Breck graduated high school, went to college, and received two degrees only to be told, more suggested, this job is not for someone like you. Breck told me one time after a job interview "Dad, I could literally feel their faces drop when I walked in with my cane." Discouraged Breck took the one outlet that she understood the best writing. She has always been a storyteller and could capture a moment better than most adults I encountered. Her mother and I suggested she tell her story. The story about the struggles with making friends and being bullied. Maybe by telling her story she could somehow heal. There is a lot of traumas in Elsie, trauma that Breck experienced firsthand, this opportunity allows Breck the opportunity to heal. While Breck is healing we hope that this book will help another person, adult or child, cope with bullying, isolation and generally just feeling left out.